What a

"*Think and Grow Rich* is one of the best financial books I have read and I commend the efforts of Elisabeth and Jan for translating the principles in Napoleon Hill's book into a story that appeals to kids. The practical, time-tested lessons illustrated in *Rocks to Riches* can help today's youth create a happy, healthy, abundant life. I encourage parents, teachers and community leaders to share *Rocks to Riches* with this generation."

Vince Shorb, CMO, National Financial Educators Council.

"Elisabeth and Jan are pros at transforming kids into money and credit smart adults. Their latest work, *Rocks to Riches*, is a creative, compelling book that the 'tween set will both learn from and enjoy. America is overdue for a new generation of financially smart citizens - and I strongly believe that *Rocks to Riches* is a powerful force in making that goal a reality."

Erica Sandberg, personal finance expert and editor-at-large for Credit Card Guide

"*Rocks to Riches* is another brilliant creation from the inspirational and genius minds of Elisabeth Donati and Jan K. Ruskin. I encourage everyone to read this magnificent story that enriches the mind and spirit."

Sam X Renick, Author, Songwriter, Financial Educator

"Empowering our kids when it comes to money and what's truly important in life is so necessary right now. Elisabeth and Jan did an amazing job of weaving nuggets of inspiration and wisdom into an adventure for kids."

Misty Gibbs, Founder, EmpowerLounge.com

# *What kids are saying...*

"*Rocks to Riches* is one of those books that reads like a good movie. It's a story that makes you feel good about people and about life!"

Jessica, 14

"Who knew a book based on rocks with writing on them would be as spectacular as this book! A book with amazing life lessons, yet with a down to earth story. If this book does not please you, I don't know what will."

Alec, 10

"I loved it! I really liked how the relationships in the story transform and develop...you really think about this whole idea about financial problems and how you can actually help yourself."

Isabel, 12

"Ace, Nan, Millie, Jack and Kara had the best adventures when they explored the world outside their home...It was such a good book that I think there should be a second book."

Maggie, 9

"I think other kids my age will love this book...it's a great book about five kids who go on a treasure hunt...and it teaches you how to reach your goals in life."

Caroline, almost 11

"It's not all about money, it's about kids enjoying summer fun, having laughs, and just hanging out with friends."

Brock, 13

"My Mum gave me a special stone that had 'Dream' written on it... I now understand that not only do I have to dream, I also have to plan, stay focused, and keep working towards my goal."

Mikaila, 9

"I loved this book and couldn't put it down! The book is very interesting... also very inspiring."

Troxell, 11

You will love it, too!

# Rocks to RICHES

by

Elisabeth Donati

and

Jan K. Ruskin

for Jodi and Maia —
May you always notice
the magic in the cracks
of the sidewalk — and
enjoy the adventures
along the way!

InnerWealth Publishing
Santa Barbara, CA

Jan & Elisabeth Donati

Published in Santa Barbara, California,
by InnerWealth Publishing.

www.RocksToRichesBook.com

Library of Congress Control Number: 2011962282

Donati, Elisabeth.
Ruskin, Jan K.

Rocks to Riches / Elisabeth Donati and Jan K. Ruskin.

Summary: Five children go on a treasure hunt and find the stepping stones to wealth.

ISBN: 978-0-9774618-4-4

Manufactured in the United States of America

# Acknowledgments


## From Elisabeth

In all of my years, I will never quite know where ideas come from…outside of us, inside of us, somewhere even deeper than we can ever think without our brains saying "Wait…I don't know how to think about that!"

The idea for this book, and hence the story that just happened, came from 'that place', as do all of my creations. I want to acknowledge my own inner knowing for being a vessel to receive from that special place.

Between the beginning and end of any creative project, there are people who help, people who support, and people who participate without ever knowing. I'm grateful to all of these people for all of these things.

To Steve, my partner now and for as long as we choose, who makes everything that comes from me better, sweeter, deeper and, well, more playful. To Jan, who decided she wanted to make the story better in the most beautifully insightful way. And thanks, finally, to my Mother who read Dr. Seuss stories to me all through my childhood because it taught me to love words dancing on a page and stories that invite children to think deeper than they might otherwise think. We all know the world needs more children who can think!

# Acknowledgments (cont.)

### From Jan

Often with a piece of art, whether a painting or a story, I have to call it "complete" or I would go on forever with its creation. I think it takes a certain amount of courage and humility to put our art in the hands of others. I hope this story is a source of delight and inspiration for those who take a look.

I want to acknowledge all the people, past and present, who help me see beyond my conditioned ways of thinking and being. Thank you to Elisabeth, for your generosity and trust in allowing me to come in and deepen what you created. To my husband, Mark, thank you for your patience and big love. To my son, Logan, your truth and wisdom. To my parents and my sister, your unending support for my expression in the world. To my stepdaughters, for letting me find my way. And to my friends, thank you for keeping it real.

### From Elisabeth and Jan

We want to acknowledge Mandy Webster for being a contributor to this work.

Thank you also to Ruth Gordon for her careful editing, Henrietta Berkers for her creative layout, Amy Musson for making sure the story made sense, KillerCovers who captured the book's essence in the cover, and for all of the other adults in our lives who have given us feedback along the way. We couldn't have done it without you.

*"Opportunity often comes disguised in the form of misfortune, or temporary defeat."*

~ Napoleon Hill

# Contents

## CHAPTER 1

# Summer Heat

"Nan, GET UP NOW!"

Nan pulled the yellow-flowered quilt over her head in one last effort to return to the morning dream-state she relished. She peeked out from under the covers to watch the shadows on her bedroom wall as the sun filtered through the window shade.

Ever since she was a little girl, she would imagine her wall to be a ballroom…the shadows dancing in competition. Nan wanted nothing more than to stay in bed and judge the contest of waltzing shadows but she knew her mother had other plans for her. She sighed and threw the blanket to the floor. Three weeks into her summer vacation and she had nothing to show for it, not even sleeping in! The only possible good part to getting up was that it would soon be stuffy in their tiny apartment and the heat would drive her outside looking for fresh air anyway.

Her mother burst through the door. "Nan, I am about to be late for work!"

"I'm up, I'm up," groaned Nan.

Ms. Webster stood with her fists on her hips and tapped an irritated toe on the hardwood floor. Her long, dark hair was pulled back in a neat bun, and her dark eyes flashed. Maureen

...ster was a force to be reckoned with in the morning. She would not let up until she got what she wanted! "Get up on your feet now, Miss Sleepy-head!"

"Okay, okay!"

"I need to know that you're awake enough to look after your sister!" Nan's mom paused at the bedroom door just long enough to smooth out the skirt of her faded pink waitress uniform and straighten her name tag. Petite and cute in a plain sort of way, Ms. Webster was equally strong and feisty.

Nan grumbled as she walked down the hall to the bathroom. She hated being 12. It was such an in-between age. She was old enough to baby sit her 5-year-old sister but too young to say "no". She wanted to make sure her mother knew exactly how she felt about it without being too obvious. Nan flipped on the light switch and heard her mother yell as the electricity throughout the entire apartment died. "Not again!" groaned Nan.

Her mother's muffled cry reached Nan through the thin walls. "What a disgrace!"

Nan brushed her teeth quickly then joined her mother in the kitchen. Ms. Webster was in the middle of an all-too-familiar rant. "Mr. Gizewski is such an idiot! Do you know how much more rent he could get if he fixed this place up just a little bit? This building is in an excellent location. If he had half the brains God gave the rats that roam these halls, he could get wealthy off this place."

"Yes, Mom, but then we couldn't afford to live here," Nan rebuked, as if on cue.

"Mark my words, Nan. Things are going to change when I own this building. I'll fix it up, throw out everything that doesn't work, and make it the best building on the block." She turned to Nan and waved her finger. "AND, make the top floor our penthouse!"

Nan rolled her eyes. She knew it would never happen. But, if the fantasy helped her mom keep a positive outlook in the dismal apartment, Nan would listen to it again. She watched her mother gather her things and head toward the door, barking orders as she went. Sometimes Nan felt like her life was a movie, with the same scene playing over and over again.

"You keep your sister with you at all times," Ms. Webster said. "And stay off the elevator!" she called as the lights flickered back on. "You don't want to get stuck in that contraption on a day like today. Stay this side of 76th and watch for cars. And don't forget your key if you leave the apartment."

Nan followed her mother to the door. She had only heard this list of rules about a million times before. "You're going to be late, Mom," she reminded her.

"Right. Have a good day, sweetie. I love you.

"I'm leaving, Kara!" she added, calling to her younger daughter. "Be good and listen to your sister."

"Bye, Mommy!" Kara replied absentmindedly, too enthralled with her television cartoon to look up.

With a whoosh, Ms. Webster was out of the apartment, and Nan closed the door behind her. She got her favorite cereal from the cupboard and trudged into the living room. She plopped into her old beanbag chair and ate her breakfast right out of the box.

"Why can't the 'lectricily go off during a commercial?" Kara asked. Her little body was sprawled across a pile of pillows amid an array of coloring books, crayons, and toys. Kara always seemed the happiest when surrounded by a mess!

"Electricity," Nan corrected her younger sister. "Give me the remote."

"No, I'm watching!" Kara replied, tucking the TV remote into her armpit.

"I don't care, I'm in charge and I'm not watching this stupid show," Nan bossed, grabbing for the remote.

Kara tried to crawl away, but Nan grabbed her foot. "It's not stupid!" she protested, wriggling a bare foot out of her sock and scurrying around the bar that divided the kitchen and living room. She peeked around the corner to see if her tormenter followed. Just then the electricity flickered off again.

"Just as well," Nan stated. She stood with her fists at her hips and tapped an impatient toe on the floor, very much like her mother had done only a few minutes before. "Go get your shoes on and comb your hair so we can go outside before we smother to death. I'm going to get dressed."

When they met back at the front door, Kara had her sandals but she also had a wide, dirt-streaked grin under a tangled halo of dark brown hair. Kara looked more like her mom than Nan did but, instead of brown eyes, had big green ones.

"Kara!" Nan glared at her in disbelief. "What did you get all over your face in the two minutes it took you to get your shoes?"

"I don't know," Kara shrugged.

Nan groaned for the umpteenth time that morning and made her way to the bathroom for a comb and washcloth. After scrubbing Kara's face, she went to work on her hair.

"Ow!" Kara protested, trying to free herself from the wrath of the dreaded comb.

"Sit still!" Nan ordered. She made two more quickly forced swipes through Kara's hair and then pushed her out of the bathroom. "Consider yourself lucky! If it were up to me, I'd chop all that hair right off!"

Nan cringed at the sound of her own voice. She sounded more like a mother than a sister, but she was so frustrated with the whole morning.

Kara stuck her tongue out and then escaped out the front door before Nan could grab her.

"Stay off the elevator!" Nan called, quickly shutting and locking the apartment door behind her. She turned just in time to see the elevator doors close on her impudent sister and ran for the stairs. Taking them two by two, she managed to reach the elevator on the ground floor just as the doors opened to reveal Kara's grinning face, which was once more smudged with dirt. "What do you do, rub your face on the floor?" Nan exclaimed in disbelief.

Kara simply grinned again and, prancing past her sister, pushed through the front door into the brilliant light of day.

Nan sighed. She had to constantly remind herself to be patient. She loved Kara because she was her sister, of course, but lately Nan saw her mostly as an annoyance *and* the main reason she wasn't having the summer she wanted.

"I'm gonna go see Jack's pig," Kara announced, skipping down the sidewalk.

Nan ran a few paces to catch up. "I don't even know if Jack's back yet," she said. "And besides, his jerky stepbrother will be there, too."

"How do you know he's a jerk?" Kara asked without losing her momentum.

" 'Cause Jack says so."

"Maybe Jack's just jealous," Kara sang out astutely. For such a little kid, Kara often seemed more aware than she should.

"Maybe," Nan answered.

She had never thought about Jack being jealous before, but it made sense. After all, he'd had his mother all to himself for three years since his father took off. Now he had to share her with a new stepfather and a stepbrother who was almost the same age as he was. Well, if he was jealous, she couldn't blame him! She couldn't imagine how she would feel if her own mother got remarried. She was pretty sure it would be awful, though.

Nan thought about her own dad, who had died when she was six. Her memories were fading more and more as she got older but she knew she had loved him and would never want someone else to take his place. Suddenly, Nan felt sad for Kara. She never even knew him.

"Alright, let's go see Jack and his pig," Nan said more sweetly. It was as good an idea as any. She would go see this new step-brother and make up her own mind about him.

The two girls skipped together down a quiet side street. The fresh air felt good and Nan's mood brightened the closer they got to Jack's house. She forgot all about being irritated with Kara, at least for the moment.

The farther away they went from the busy street where their own apartment building was located, the bigger and nicer the houses got. The neat little ranch house where Jack lived was somewhere near the middle between Nan's neighborhood downtown and the thick glade where the biggest houses stood in a row. Nan imagined them as haughty old women, glaring down their pointy noses at the rest of the world.

Millie Medlin lived in one of the mini-mansions that bordered the woods. Nan had known Millie since Kindergarten but they had never been true friends. Millie was the kind of girl who could be very sweet when she wanted something but, as soon as she got her way, she couldn't care less about you.

The problem was that Millie's and Jack's moms were best friends so, if Nan wanted to hang out with Jack, she had to put up with Millie as well. Not to mention the fact that they were pretty much the only other kids her age in the entire neighborhood.

As if her thoughts had sent out an invitation, a bright red convertible swooped into Jack's driveway just as Nan and Kara approached. Nan groaned as she watched Millie take off her scarf and smooth out her glossy blond hair. Nan's own hair was just a regular dark blond and she longed for sun-kissed highlights. Her mom refused to even talk about it until she turned 13 – another reason why 12 was not so great.

"I guess Jack's back," Nan said to no one in particular.

Millie's mom hoisted herself up to sit on the edge of her car door. "Good morning, girls!" She looked over the top of her designer sunglasses and peered down at them, wrinkling her perfect little nose in distaste at the sight of Kara's dirt-streaked face. "Where are you heading today?" she asked.

Linda Lee Medlin always looked like a movie star with her perfectly-groomed blond hair and just-manicured nails. Her long, shapely legs stepped from the car. She wore shorts and high-heeled sandals and looked like a total knock-out, as usual.

"We're gonna see Jack's pig!" Kara answered, grinning from ear to ear.

Nan glanced at her sister's smudged face and tangled hair and was reminded of her earlier irritation with her. Nan was forever embarrassed and liked to fantasize that she was secretly stolen from a cultured, upper crust family who was somewhere searching for their beloved missing daughter.

"We just came to see how Jack's vacation went," said Nan, not sure if going on your own mother's honeymoon could be called a vacation.

Millie looked into the mirror on the back of the car's sun visor and smoothed her hair again before stepping out onto the driveway. She was a younger, smaller version of her mother right down to their matching shorts and heeled sandals. Judging by those shoes, Nan guessed there would be no outdoor activities with her friends that morning.

"You better go see Jack's pig quick before it's bacon!" Millie exclaimed. She liked to gloat whenever she knew something before anyone else. "He tore up the entire kitchen while Jack was gone and now Mrs. Metter…I mean, Mrs. Emerson, is ready to ship him off to the nearest meat packing plant!"

Kara looked horrified at the prospect and ran to find Chubbs, the potbellied pig.

"He's probably out back!" Millie called behind her. She turned to look down her nose at Nan and grinned. "Have you met Ace yet? He's sooo cute!"

"I heard he was a jerk," Nan dismissed. Nevertheless, she followed Millie and Kara around the side of the house while Mrs. Medlin went in through the front door.

"Who cares about that?" Millie said, trying to sound worldly. "Cute is cute." She took Nan by the hand and dragged her into the back yard to show her just how cute Jack's new stepbrother was. It was only Jack, though, who was there in the makeshift pen where poor Chubbs was now incarcerated.

Jack looked up at the girls with watery eyes and sniffled. Nan wasn't sure if he had been crying or if it was merely his overly militant allergies attacking as usual. An abrupt sneeze appeared to answer her question. The scrawny boy wiped his nose with the back of his hand and adjusted his glasses. His curly brown hair was in disarray as usual, and Nan thought that he looked like an absent-minded professor more than ever. Jack wore knee-high socks with his sandals and had a smear of white sun block across the top of one of his already peeling cheeks. Nan had nothing but compassion, though, as Jack was purely one of the nicest people she knew.

"Oh, poor Chubbsie Wubbs!" Kara crooned, scratching the unlikely pet between his ears. He leaned into her as though he thought he were a small dog. He obviously had no idea that he weighed at least twice as much as Kara, if not more. Chubbs was kind of cute, but was fatter than the last time Nan had seen him. His back was starting to sway with the gravity of his belly, which jiggled as he pushed even closer to his most adoring fan.

"Be careful he doesn't step on your toes," Nan reminded her sister.

"Ugh, how can you stand it?" Millie asked. "I don't know how your mother let that smelly thing stay in the house for so long."

"Chubbs does not smell," Jack informed her indignantly. "For your information, potbellieds are very clean animals."

Millie only giggled and pinched her nose. "He's still a pig!"

Nan climbed into the new pen that had been built since her last visit. "Has Chubbs really been kicked out of the house for good?"

"Yeess!" Jack wailed. "But, it's not his fault! None of this would have ever happened if I'd been home! It's not Chubbs' fault the neighbor got busy and forgot to feed him! What was he supposed to do, starve?"

"What did he do?" Nan asked.

"Oh, he only destroyed the entire kitchen!"

Nan turned in the direction of an unfamiliar voice. She assumed that the boy walking toward the group was none other than Jack's new stepbrother, Ace Emerson. He approached with the characteristic swagger of any stereotypical sports jock. And he *was* cute! He had a short, neat haircut with a cowlick that sent one lock of his black hair falling on his forehead. He had a glint in his eye and a cocky grin that left Nan feeling as though he could read her every thought.

"That pig got into every cabinet door he could nudge open and ate every scrap of food he could find," Ace continued. "Then he cleaned out the refrigerator! You should have seen it! Unbelievable! There were bags and boxes and containers ripped open everywhere...even chocolate pudding on the ceiling fan!"

Jack's face grew red. "That's ridiculous," he retorted. "You don't know anything." Ace went on. "I *do* know that your mom was ready to take my dad's service pistol and put a bullet through the pigster's skull right then and there! Oh, hey Millie." Ace switched gears and winked at the girls while he laughed heartily and leaned over the fence to give Chubbs a swift smack on the rump.

"Hey," he said to Kara. "What's your name?"

"I'm Kara! Who are you?"

"Don't touch my pig!" Jack growled between gritted teeth before continuing the story where Ace left off. "Meanwhile, this moron over here is laughing his stupid head off so hard, he was practically rolling around on the floor! A big help you were!"

Ace laughed. "It's true," he said. "I laughed so hard I swear I almost peed my pants! It was the funniest thing I ever saw in my life!"

While Nan could imagine the hilarity of the scene described, her loyalty to her friend squashed the giggle that threatened to bubble up. Ace was getting a lot of enjoyment at Jack's expense and Nan thought he was being awfully mean in front of people he had just met. Just then, Kara erupted in a giggle of her own, and Nan smiled despite herself. Ace gave her a lopsided grin, and she had to turn away to keep from joining in.

Not to be overlooked, Millie inserted herself between Nan and Ace. "Hi, Ace," she said breathlessly. "How was your vacation?" Millie leaned against the fence and looked up at him over her sunglasses.

"It was okay," Ace answered nonchalantly. "They had an awesome rock-climbing wall right on the cruise ship! But it would have been a lot more fun if my dad didn't make me hang out with this loser the whole time. All he wanted to do was sit on the deck and read books all day or catalog sea life in his little girly diary."

Jack sneered at Ace's derisive description of him. "It's a *field journal*," he informed him. "And we can't all be dumb jocks with no intellectual matter between our ears like you."

"Whatever, dude," Ace shrugged him off.

"What was it like going on a *honeymoon*?" Millie inquired vapidly. "I would have been so weirded out. Did they make out and stuff the whole time?"

"Nah," Ace said, clearly getting bored with the subject. "Who are you?" he asked, sidestepping Millie.

"Um, I'm Nan," she replied shyly.

"Cool, what grade are you in?"

Nan could see Millie shifting about awkwardly behind Ace's back, trying to figure out the best way to force her way back into the spotlight. She was clearly not amused that he had turned his attentions to Nan.

"I'm going into Sixth, like Jack and Millie. Are you?"

"Looks like it," Ace said. "My dad just sold our house on the South side, so I guess we're moving in here permanently." The thought didn't seem to thrill him.

"I'm gonna be in First Grade!" Kara piped up.

"No, you're not," said Nan. "You're going into Kindergarten."

"I know!" she admitted coyly.

"Hey, that's cool!" Ace said to Kara.

He seemed nice enough to Kara so Nan reminded herself not to jump to any conclusions.

"Jack, please!" Mrs. Emerson called impatiently from the back door of the garage. "I need you to go through this stuff quickly so I can haul it off to the second-hand store on the way to lunch with Linda Lee. Let's get a move-on!"

Jack scowled as he trudged from Chubbs' pen and into the garage. Millie, Nan, and Kara started to follow him but Millie hung back when she realized that Ace wasn't coming as well. "So, what do you want to do today?" she asked him, obviously planning to spend the entire day with the new boy in town.

Ace stepped past Millie. "I'm game to see what kind of mess Jack is into." Ace hurried to follow them to the garage. Nan figured Millie's attention was a little too much for Ace. Millie was pretty, but she was also intense.

Millie ran after Ace to joined them in the dark garage. It took a few seconds for their eyes to adjust to the dim light.

"What is all this junk?" Millie queried.

"It's not junk!" Jack stated. "This is a bunch of my dad's stuff. Ace's dad is making my mom throw it out so he can put *his* stuff in the garage."

"Hey, it was your mom's idea," Ace said, defending his father.

"Yeah, but I could keep my dad's stuff here forever if it weren't for your dad!" Jack argued. He stood with his arms crossed and pouted.

"You're so lame," Ace told him. "This is all junk! If you ask me, your dad took everything with him that was worth having when he left."

Nan's jaw dropped. Ace could not have said anything meaner. Knowing Jack had to live with someone like that made Nan feel sick. She moved closer to Jack to make sure there was no doubt whose side she was on.

Jack clenched his fists and looked like he was ready to haul off and let Ace have it.

Nan thought she'd better do something to diffuse Jack's anger, though, because he'd be no match for the much more athletic Ace. She reached out to pick up a golf club. "Here, let me help you," she offered. She continued picking up items, hoping to distract Jack. It worked.

Jack turned his back on Ace, who thankfully didn't say anything else.

"Do you really have to get rid of everything?" asked Nan.

"No," said Jack, "my mom said I could keep a couple of things as long as they fit in my room without making too much of a mess."

"Come on, I'll help you decide what to keep," Nan said. She looked at Jack tenderly. The pile of junk and the tree house that his father had built right before he left, were obviously all he had left of their relationship. And poor, imprisoned Chubbs, Jack's beloved pig, had been a consolation gift from his mother to try to make him feel better about the abrupt abandonment.

Jack was biting his lip the way he did when he got emotional. Nan had seen him do it before and she was sure that he would rather die than shed a tear in front of his new stepbrother. He probably hated everything about Ace, especially that he had his dad. It didn't occur to Nan that Ace didn't have his own mom with him.

"What's this?" Kara asked, struggling to hold up a heavy, tangled piece of metal.

Nan was glad for Kara's added diversion.

"That," Jack answered, "is my dad's old French horn. I snuck it outside one time when I was little to try to play it. My mom called out the front door for me to come inside and I dropped it behind the van so she wouldn't see what I was doing."

"Let me guess, it got run over!" Ace stated, trying not to laugh.

Jack shrugged his shoulder and ignored Ace, turning his back on him while he directed his narration to the girls. "I ran into the house figuring I'd sneak back out after a while to get it but I didn't know my dad was coming out through the garage at the same time. He got in the van to leave and backed right over his horn!"

"Was he mad?" Kara asked with eyes wide.

"He was *so* mad!" Jack replied. "I thought I'd be grounded forever! But the next week, he started building my tree house, and well..." He trailed off as if something had just occurred to him, and then said resolutely, "Toss it."

Kara began to lug the heavy piece of metal to the front of the garage where Mrs. Emerson began to load everything into the back of her van. Mrs. Medlin stood to the side, chattering away while Jack's mom kept working. Nan didn't understand people like that.

"That thing can just go right in the garbage," Mrs. Emerson told Kara, reaching to take the battered French horn from her. Jack sighed and turned back to the pile of junk his friends were picking through. Nan thought there must something worth keeping.

"This old bowl is kinda cool," Nan said, picking up a tarnished piece of metal.

Jack reached to take it from her. "This is no bowl, Nan," he told her. "This is a pan that people used to use when they were looking for gold up in the hills."

"Let me see that!" Millie grabbed greedily for the pan. "How can this old hunk of metal find gold?"

Jack explained, "Back in the old days, people would take something like this and use it to pan for gold in the streams. They could sift the gold from the sand and rocks and just walk away with it. They didn't even need to own a mine to get rich, as long as they didn't get on somebody else's land!"

"Really…" Millie said thoughtfully.

Nan could see the wheels turning in her head.

"Do you think we could find gold with it now?" asked Millie.

"Sure," Jack told her. "I mean, theoretically, anyway. There's no telling if there is any gold left to find. But it's possible more has washed down from the hills since people stopped looking for it. That was a long time ago, after all."

"So, we can just take this old pan out to the stream behind my house and pick gold right up out of the water?" Millie asked breathlessly.

"I guess so," Jack shrugged. "I guess I never really thought about it."

"Of course *you* wouldn't," Millie told him. She stood looking into the pan as if she could see her reflection looking back at her with a crown upon her golden head. "What do you say we try?" she asked, cocking her head to one side with an unmistakable gleam in her eye.

"I guess we could," Jack replied, always eager to please the beautiful Millie.

"Let's go then!" said Millie.

"Wait just one minute!" Mrs. Emerson interrupted them. "Jack, you aren't going anywhere until this mess is cleaned up."

Jack glanced back and forth between an impatient Millie and the rusting pile of rubble on the garage floor and quickly came to a decision. "Let's just toss it all," he said resolutely.

And with that, they began to pile all of the junk into the van and the garbage bin. All, that is, except for the gold pan, which Millie clung to like it was gold itself.

CHAPTER 2

# Looking for Gold

"Stay out of trouble!" Mrs. Emerson called to Jack as she and Mrs. Medlin backed out of the driveway in the shiny convertible. Nan thought most parents were overly concerned about the trouble kids could get into. What possible trouble could there be in such a small, dull town?

Jack's mom called out one more time. "And, don't you dare let that pig back in the house!"

Nan watched Jack roll his eyes as he always did when his mom talked about Chubbs. He stalked off toward his captive pet in the back yard and the others followed. Well, except for Millie who seemed anxious to get to the gold mine in the woods.

"Can we just go now and stop worrying about that dumb pig?" Millie asked impatiently.

"I have to make sure Chubbs has water, then we can go," Jack indulged her. Millie groaned but followed anyway.

Jack stopped short and surveyed the pen. "This just isn't right," he said, bemoaning the circumstances of his fat old companion. "There's no shade here at all! Chubbs is going to be totally sunburned by the end of the day!"

"Are you saying you don't like your bacon burned?" Ace joked.

Jack glared at his stepbrother but didn't reply. He looked around the yard trying to think of a better place to put Chubbs.

"Why can't we just take Chubbs with us?" Kara asked.

Ace snorted, trying to hold back his hearty laugh. His attempted restraint was merely met with another glare, this time from Millie.

"That's just dumb," Millie said. "That stupid thing is only going to get in our way. Let's just go! Mr. Emerson wouldn't have built his pen here if he didn't think it would be okay."

"I wouldn't be so sure of that," Jack said.

"What's that supposed to mean?" Ace scowled.

"Only that your dad doesn't know a thing about pigs or what they need...unless you count the 'pigs' that he works with."

"I told you, don't call my dad a pig!" Ace stood up to his full height, towering over Jack's slight frame. "He's a detective, and..."

"Is there any reason why Chubbs couldn't go along with us?" Nan interrupted, ever the diplomat. "He doesn't try to run away or anything, does he?"

"If only!" Ace nearly spat the words out.

"No," Jack replied meekly, and then brightened. "Let's do it...let's take him with us!"

"Well, whatever we're doing, can we go already?!" Millie grew more impatient with each passing second. Nan could almost see the dollar signs flashing in her pale blue eyes.

Jack opened Chubbs' pen and called him out. "Let's go!" he said.

"Finally!" Millie said, stalking away. "We have to stop by my house first so I can grab a different pair of shoes. And that *thing* is not coming in!"

"Come on, Chubbsie!" Kara sang, skipping ahead of Millie and into the street.

"Watch for cars!" Nan cried, exasperated. She ran to catch up with Kara. She absolutely did not like being responsible for someone else. It was too much pressure.

Ace hung back for a moment, looking as if he couldn't decide what to do. Nan couldn't blame him – nice air conditioning and a TV or a bunch of people he barely knew. She found herself smiling when he ran to catch up to them.

"How far is it to your house?" Ace asked Millie.

"It's just a couple of blocks down the street, and then the woods are right in our back yard. We have the best view in the entire neighborhood," she boasted.

Nan began to slow her pace as she contemplated how Ace's addition to their group might change things. If one thing changed, maybe other things would, too. Maybe the summer wouldn't be a total loss after all.

Before she knew it, Ace caught up and fell into step with her. "Where do you live?" he asked.

"We're in one of those apartment buildings over on 76th," Nan replied.

"Oh, those are nice," Ace told her. "Well, except for that one old eyesore right in the middle. My dad says if they'd tear that place down, the property values would shoot up throughout the entire neighborhood."

"Yeah, well, we live in the eyesore," Nan mumbled.

Ace's face flushed a bright red. "I'm sorry," he stumbled over his words. "I mean, well..."

"Don't worry about it," Nan said, saving him from more embarrassment. That was the last thing she wanted to talk about anyway. "Let's go catch up with the others," she said.

Nan lengthened her stride to fall into step with Millie and Jack, who were intently discussing the best place to start panning for gold. They reached Millie's house before they could come to a consensus, and Millie felt around under a nearby window ledge for the spare key.

"You don't seriously keep a key right there, do you?" Ace asked, appalled. "My dad is a cop...do you know how easy it would be for someone to get into your house with a key hidden in the most obvious place?"

Millie merely shrugged and opened the front door. Walking into the entryway of the Medlin house was like stepping into an icebox compared to Nan's stuffy apartment. The Medlins obviously didn't give much thought to the huge amount of energy it took to cool their gigantic home.

"Wow, nice place!" Ace said, gazing up at the vaulted ceiling.

Millie ran up the staircase that wound up the curved wall of the huge entryway. "I'll just change my shoes and be right back," she said. "Jack, don't let that stupid pig in the house!"

Jack grumbled and stepped back outside with Chubbs and Kara. Ace continued his appraisal of the Medlin home. "Wow, they must be loaded!" he said.

Nan rolled her eyes. "You think?"

"Jealous?"

This time it was Nan's turn to blush. "Of course not!" She spat over her shoulder as she turned on her heel and stalked outside. Even if she was jealous, it was none of Ace's business. Besides, who wouldn't want all that money? Millie could have everything she wanted.

"Yeah right," Ace mumbled to himself, following Nan out the door and back into the sticky heat.

A moment later, Millie joined them outside and led them around behind her house. Ace gazed longingly at the in ground pool. "Awesome pool," he called out to no one in particular. He lagged behind but caught up with the others just as they stepped into the cool shade of the woods behind Millie's house.

"Do you really think there's still gold in the stream?" Nan was skeptical as she followed Millie and Jack down the narrow path through the woods.

Ace dragged his feet in the dirt and grumbled behind them. "This is stupid," he mumbled to himself. "Let's go back to Millie's and swim," he said. He kicked a rock down the hill, which ricocheted off of Nan's shoe. She looked back and glared at him. Cute, maybe, but definitely annoying.

Jack wiped the sweat from his brow with the back of his hand and pushed his glasses back into place. "Most of the gold in this area was found in the river," he lectured, "but no one ever found its source. The gold has to come from somewhere. I bet it still washes down the river even today. Anything is possible."

"Oh, can you just imagine what we'll do with all that gold?" Millie said, breathlessly. Her eyes glazed over and her feet came to an abrupt halt. Ace was still kicking rocks like he was playing soccer and bumped right into her.

"You scuffed my new shoes!" Millie scowled. Her designer tennis shoes were only slightly more appropriate for the woods than her heeled sandals.

Ace's cheeks flushed and Nan smiled to herself. "Let's just keep moving," said Nan. Ace shrugged and Millie flounced away with a huff. The heat seemed to be making everyone grumpy.

Kara was unaffected, though, and was happily running back and forth on the path with Chubbs. "Are we really gonna find gold?" she called.

"We're gonna try," said Jack. He smiled at Kara and hoisted the pan up onto his shoulder, trying to find a more comfortable way to carry it. It hadn't appeared very heavy at all when they left his house, but now it seemed to grow heavier with every step he took.

Of course, it never occurred to Millie to take a turn lugging the thing. Jack knew it was Millie's way, though, and mostly overlooked it. He probably knew Millie better than anyone else and seemed to forgive her, a lot. Nan had heard Jack say, "She was just born that way." Nan wondered if that were true, if people were just born a certain way and couldn't be any different no matter what they did.

The haggard group hiked on along the sun-dappled path, starting to melt into the coolness of the forest on the hot day. They could hear the faint gurgling of the stream hidden in the woods ahead of them. After a few more minutes of walking, the trees began to thin and, before they knew it, the stream appeared in front of them. The sun glinted on the water as it flowed over the bumpy bottom of stones, sanded smooth by the swift water.

Chubbs surged down the hill, comically leaping over the last few feet of dirt and into the water. Kara tripped down the bank of the stream, joyfully splashing right in after him, shoes and all.

"Kara, sheesh!" Nan exclaimed. "Take your shoes off first!" She groaned, knowing that she would be the one to have to answer to their mother for the ruined shoes, not her little sister.

Kara scrambled onto a large rock near the edge of the water and rushed to pull her shoes off, throwing them toward Nan.

"A lot of good that does!" scolded Nan.

Kara hopped back in, splashing her hot feet in the cool, clear water with glee. Nan couldn't help but smile a little, partly enjoying and partly envying Kara's pure delight.

Millie stood on the bank with her hands on her hips and turned up the end of her prim little nose. "Okay, Jack," she said matter-of-factly. "What do we do first?" She didn't normally like to get her fingernails dirty, but with this much gold on the line, it seemed she was ready to work.

Jack took a pair of water shoes from his ever-present backpack and waded carefully into the stream with his gold pan full of sand and rocks and began to swirl it around. "Gold is heavier than other rocks and stuff," he explained, "so it settles in the sand alongside rivers and streams like this one. First you dip the pan under the water and scoop up the bottom like this," he demonstrated. Jack was at his best when he was sharing information.

"You lift it just to the surface of the water and swirl it around while tipping it so the lighter materials float out over the side. Just keep adding water a little at a time and swirling it around until most of the rocks and stuff fall out. Eventually, all you have left is some sand and hopefully a lot of gold flakes!"

Nan admired Jack. He really was a nerd…lovable…but a total and complete nerd!

Millie took off her shoes, tossing them carelessly along the shoreline. She stepped delicately into the stream and peered into Jack's gold pan. "I don't see any gold," she stated with disappointment.

Jack just looked at Millie. "Well, it could take a little while," he said.

Millie shrugged.

Meanwhile, Nan flipped her sandals off and sat on the big rock to dabble her feet in the stream. She relaxed back on her elbows and watched Ace who was farther downstream. He peeled off his shirt and did a cannon ball into a deep pool. "Woo-hoo!" he yelped, coming up for air. "The water's a lot colder than it looks!"

With a sideways glance at Millie, who was hard at work watching Jack hard at work, Nan pushed herself up from the rock and went in to join her sister. The rocks crunched as they scraped together beneath her feet, and the sun warmed her damp knees. She half listened to her sister's chattering as she trailed the tips of her fingers in the stream and eyed the smooth stones under the water's clear surface. She blocked out the irritating sound of Millie berating Jack for taking so long to find her gold.

Nan's mind drifted with the current. She thought of what she would do if she found gold. She tried to think of something really frivolous, but her thoughts always returned to her mother. When it came right down to it, Nan admired her mom. She knew how hard her mom worked. Day after day, her mom waited on tables and did accounting on the side. That, plus everything else she did for Nan and Kara. "A car..." Nan thought. "If I found gold, I would buy my mom a car first thing. And a vacation... for all of us!"

Just then she noticed a faint glint beneath the surface of the water. It disappeared for a moment and then reappeared in another brief flash. Nan inched forward, careful not to stir up any mud. There it was again, that tiny flash of light as the sun glinted off of something lying at the bottom of the stream. Nan's breathing almost stopped as she bent down and reached her hand into the water to pick up the rock.

"What'd you find?" Ace startled Nan, as she turned to find him right at her elbow. She opened her hand and the two of them stared at the big glittering object lying in her palm. Suddenly, Ace grabbed the rock and started jumping up and down in the water. "Hey, you guys! Look!" he cried. "Nan found it! She found the gold!"

Jack and Millie froze and then Millie almost knocked Jack off his feet as she pushed past him trying to get to Nan and Ace first. Ace held the rock out in his hand for her to see, and she snatched it away.

"I'm rich, I'm rich!" Millie exclaimed, jumping in the water just as Ace had only a few seconds before. "I'm gonna buy a pony and a tiara! No, two tiaras...one for me and one for my pony!"

She was being positively goofy, thought Nan.

Ace grabbed Millie's hand trying to pry the rock from her iron grip. "What do you mean you're rich?" he asked. "Nan found it, not you!"

Nan looked from Ace's snarling face to Millie's mud-smudged pout and laughed in disbelief just as Jack trudged up and reached for the gold in Millie's hand. "Let me see that," he said. Millie handed the stone to Jack, knowing that she would have no problem getting it back from him. They all turned to Jack and held their breath, waiting for him to tell them how much money the gold would bring them. Jack held the rock up to the light for only an instant before rolling his eyes and handing it back to Millie. "Iron pyrite," he stated simply.

"What?" the other three asked in unison.

"Iron pyrite," Jack replied. "Fool's gold, not real gold."

"What?!" Millie exclaimed again as she grabbed the rock.

"It's not gold," Jack told her again. "It's just a rock that looks like gold. They call it fool's gold because a lot of people mistake it for real gold."

"How do you know this stuff?" Nan asked.

Before Jack could reply, Millie threw the rock into the stream with a violent splash. "Stupid rock!" she shouted. "You and your dumb ideas, Jack!"

As usual, Millie overreacted. She stomped up the bank and began to shove her feet angrily into her shoes. Jack merely shrugged and went to pick up his gold pan. To him, Millie was just being Millie.

Nan wondered, though, why Millie would be so upset about not finding gold. If Millie really wanted anything, even a pony, all she had to do was ask her father. Nan felt sure that Millie's father would even buy her two ponies if she asked him to. There was no doubt in Nan's mind that Millie's dad would do whatever she wanted.

"Well, it was fun to try," Nan said. "I guess if there were lots of gold, we wouldn't be the only ones out here."

Kara splashed through the stream in the direction that Millie had tossed the stone.

"Kara! What are you doing?" Nan asked, exasperated.

"I want to take that pretty rock home."

Nan knew her sister would not be satisfied until she had her pretty rock, so she went in to help. Ace followed along as well. It was Ace who found the rock again and held it out to Kara who smiled gratefully and clenched it to her chest.

Nan was the last to step up on the riverbank, and she noticed her sister looking at the rock strangely. "What's wrong?" she asked.

"There are words on my rock," Kara answered. "Nan, read it!"

Nan took the stone. She hadn't noticed before that one side of the rock was perfectly smooth with a tiny engraving of letters. She wasn't sure this was even the original stone she had found.

"Let me see that," said Ace, grabbing it from Nan and reading the words out loud.

– Know Your Desire –

"What does it mean?" Kara asked.

Nan smiled at her sister. "Maybe it's some kind of message."

Jack jumped in. "Desire means wanting," he said.

"And know means know!" Ace laughed. "Get it? No means no!"

Nan laughed but Jack continued without missing a beat. "If we know what we want," he said, "then it should be easier to get it. So maybe we need to make a statement about our desire to find gold!"

"Okay, I have a statement!" said Millie, sarcastically. "We KNOW we desire gold!"

"I don't think that's exactly it, Millie," said Jack.

"Me, too," said Kara. "I want gold!"

Ace snorted. "Let's go to the pool so I can get to know my desire to swim!"

"Me, too," said Kara. "I want to swim!"

"Looks like you already did!" joked Ace.

Jack rolled his eyes but Nan was suddenly having fun. "Well, I guess we all know what we want!" she laughed. She didn't even care that Kara was streaked with dirt once more.

* * * * *

Nan had already given Kara a bath and put her to bed by the time Ms. Webster finally put her key in the lock that evening. She was curled up in her beanbag chair, scribbling away in her journal about the day's events when her mother walked in.

Obviously, her mom was worn out. Not only had she worked twelve hours straight that day, but she had probably walked the mile home, too.

Ms. Webster kicked her shoes off and collapsed onto the couch.

"You want something to eat?" Nan asked.

"No, I ate at the restaurant," Ms. Webster glanced into the kitchen area and groaned. "Would it have been too much for you to wash up after dinner?"

Nan couldn't believe that was the first thing her mom noticed. "Kara is *such* a pain! She was climbing the walls all night and totally driving me crazy! All you see is what I don't do."

A knowing smile crept into the corners of Ms. Webster's mouth, but she was too exhausted to put much effort into it. "You're right," she said. "I'm sorry. I know watching Kara can be a full-time job. But those dishes are going to have to be washed tonight, or it's an open invitation for every rat in the building to come bunk with us." She started to push herself up from the couch.

"No, Mom, I'll do them," Nan told her mother, suddenly feeling more generous.

"Thank you, baby. You have no idea how tired my feet are right now."

"I know," Nan mumbled. She really did want to be a help to her mom but there was not one thing she liked about washing dishes. Nan complained to herself as she cleaned up the kitchen. "I bet Millie doesn't ever have to wash dishes. She probably has a maid to do it for her. Must be nice!"

Once the kitchen was clean, Ms. Webster patted the worn couch cushion beside her, inviting her daughter to sit. She placed a weary arm over her shoulder and pulled her close. Nan enjoyed the rare opportunity to snuggle with her mom without her pesky sister butting in. A part of her felt like she was too old to cuddle up to her mother, but another part wished she could stay there forever.

Ms. Webster stroked her daughter's hair. "I know you don't like having to take care of your sister and clean the house," she said, "but I really do need your help to keep things running smoothly right now. I promise, things will get better…and, someday, you might actually thank me for raising you to be so responsible and independent."

Nan kept her reservations to herself. She couldn't imagine ever thanking her mother for raising her in near-poverty as opposed to how Millie was being raised.

"You know, Nan," her mother continued. "All of this cooking, washing, and cleaning? It's all basic Cinderella stuff." She whispered into Nan's ear, "You know, the stuff fairy tales are made of."

Nan rolled her eyes. Sometimes she marveled at her mother's ability to continue to believe in fairy tales even after all of the bad things that had happened in her life. She, herself, vowed to live a much more practical life. Her motto would be, "If I don't expect anything, I will never get disappointed." Yep, that about summed it up for Nan. She didn't want to see her own hopes dashed as her mother's had been so often.

Nan's mom sank a little further into the sofa cushions. "Do you think anyone would have ever heard of Cinderella if she'd been your basic, run of the mill princess?" she asked. "Would it be such a good story if she had been born into the lap of luxury and then grew up to marry a prince?"

"I guess not," mumbled Nan.

"You're darn right it wouldn't. It's easy to grow up to be rich when you're born rich. History is full of people who grew up and made their own way, though. It's a far greater thing to come from nothing and turn it into something, don't you think?"

"I guess so," Nan yawned. She sat up, ready for bed.

"Remember, Nan, being broke is a temporary financial condition, being poor is a state of mind. When you are poor in your mind, you are constantly weighed down with the embarrassment of your financial situation. Don't ever see our situation as an obstacle, Lovey," Ms. Webster advised. "Sometimes opportunity comes wrapped in a clever guise of adversity."

Nan yawned again, not sure if she would ever get the "poor" out of her mind.

## CHAPTER 3

# A Silver Lining

The next morning, Nan was polishing off a box of chocolate cereal when the phone rang. "Hello?" she mumbled through a mouth full of crumbs.

"Nan!" Jack sounded excited, and Nan perked up a bit.

"Hey, what's up?"

"Are you coming over today?"

"Yeah, I guess so," Nan replied.

"Millie found out Ace's dad has a metal detector and she wants to go hunting for old coins out in the woods," Jack spoke quickly.

"What the heck is her sudden interest in looking for money?"

"I don't know, but she's waiting for us at her house, and she just called to tell me I'd better hurry up."

"Let her wait!" Nan said. "I'm not even dressed yet!"

"Yeah, but..." Jack trailed off.

"I'm not rushing over there to suit Princess Millie," Nan told Jack. "I'll be there when I get there. I'll meet you at your house."

"Okay, then," Jack conceded.

Nan was sure the prospect of keeping Millie waiting didn't appeal to him but she was not going to be pushed around by the likes of Millie. She hung up, and went to pry Kara away from the TV.

Kara bounced happily in her big sister's beanbag chair, clenching a fistful of cereal and belting out the theme song to her favorite cartoon show. Nan gave her a slight shove. "Go get dressed," she said.

Kara stuck her tongue out but obediently complied. "Where are we going?" she asked Nan on her way to their bedroom.

"Millie's taking us on another wild treasure hunt."

"Yippee! I like treasure!"

Nan pulled on a pair of old cut-off jeans and a sparkly tank top. She considered her flip flops but then decided instead on a pair of ratty, old running shoes. Finally ready, Nan turned to find that her sister had decided on a frilly dress, a plastic crown, and flowery snow boots.

"Do you really think that's a good outfit to wear in the woods?"

"Yup!" Kara replied. She ran from their shared bedroom and made a beeline toward the front door. Kara ran everywhere, even if it was just to cross the room!

"Not so fast!" Nan followed her. "I am not going anywhere with you dressed like that!"

Nan chased Kara around the living room, finally pinning her down on the floor. She dragged her back to their bedroom and started digging through the dresser.

"I wanna wear this!" Kara pouted. She sat on the edge of the bed, almost defeated. "Why can't I wear a dress?"

"You can't go running around in that dress!" Nan grumbled, tossing a pair of shorts at her sister.

"But I wanna be pretty like Millie!"

Nan, who could sympathize with that notion, softened a bit. She dug around and pulled out a little skirt and a pair of leggings. "Here," she told Kara. "Now, let's see if we can find a pretty shirt to go with that, and you can keep the crown."

Satisfied, Kara ran to the bathroom and managed to run a comb through her own curls, bypassing the usual morning hair-pulling. The two girls were ready in record time, and Kara even followed Nan down the stairs and out of the apartment building.

Nan held Kara's hand and skipped with her, enjoying the sunny morning weather. A block from Jack's house, Kara ran ahead to ring the doorbell. Ace answered just as Nan arrived.

"Hey," he said, giving them a genuine smile. "Jack left. Millie has been calling here all morning."

"Oh," Nan replied. "I guess we'll just go find them, then."

Ace glanced around the empty house, and returned his gaze to Nan. "I might as well go, too. Nothing much to do around here anyway."

"Yeah, come play with us!" Kara exclaimed.

"Cool," Ace said. "Nice crown," he said to Kara.

"Thanks!" Kara grabbed Ace by the hand and dragged him down the front walk behind her. Nan followed slowly. She suddenly found herself feeling a little nervous and was glad Kara was there to fill the silence.

Kara clutched Ace's hand tightly and babbled on about nothing. Ace glanced over his shoulder and gave Nan a shrug and a wink. Her stomach fluttered.

Soon the three passed Millie's house and were stepping once again into the cool, shady woods. Kara squealed as a squirrel scampered by. She let go of Ace to chase it down the path, one hand holding her crown in place.

"Which way do you think they went?" Ace asked.

"The path kinda winds around in a circle and eventually leads back around here," Nan replied. "I doubt they went very far from it, so we can probably go either way and find them."

"I've already seen the stream, so let's go the other way," Ace decided. "Anyway, your sister's already gone that way and doesn't seem to be in any hurry to turn back!"

Nan laughed. "She likes to go her own way, that's for sure."

The two walked along in silence, only once in awhile calling ahead to Kara to make sure she was still close by. The sunlight shining between the leaves fell warmly on their heads and shoulders. Ace took off his baseball cap and wiped the sweat forming across his brow. Nan glanced at him out of the corner of her eye. He really was cute, and not as bad as Jack might think. She fought to think of something witty to say, sensing that Ace liked to laugh.

Suddenly, Nan was jolted out of her quiet reverie by the sound of a horrible squeal. She looked at Ace, startled, and then they both broke into a run. Nan's heart pounded as she tried to imagine what could have made such a gut-wrenching scream. It didn't quite sound human, but she couldn't be sure. There it was again, growing louder and more insistent. Ace ran a few steps ahead of her, but she felt a flash of pride in being able to keep up with him. Her thoughts returned to the awful squealing. The faster they ran, the louder the sound grew.

Ace came to an abrupt halt and Nan almost bowled him over. He leaned forward, hands on his knees as he tried to catch his breath. He looked down the hill in front of them and began to laugh, his loud guffaws choking in between gasping breaths. Nan stopped and stared at him, puzzled. Ace lost his balance, falling on his behind. He glanced at Nan's worried face, laughing even harder, and pointed down the hill.

Nan dragged her attention away from Ace's sideshow, and her eyes finally fell to the main event. At the bottom of the hill, in a narrow ditch, was Chubbs standing belly deep in a mud trap, squealing, literally, like the stuck pig he was. Jack stood knee-deep in the mud at Chubbs' head, trying to coax him onto dry ground. Millie, covered head to toe in mud, was sprawled on her backside, crying, with a concerned Kara hovering over her.

Nan shoved past Ace and ran down the hill. "What happened?" she cried. "Are you okay, Millie?"

"She's fine!" Jack exclaimed. "But Chubbs is stuck pretty good. Come help me."

"I am not fine!" Millie answered. "Look at me, Jack Metter! Look what your stupid pig did to me!"

Ace cantered down the hill toward the others. "This is so awesome!" he laughed. Jack and Millie both glared at him.

"What's so awesome about it?" Millie yelled at him. "You think you're so funny, you big jerk! Who even invited you, anyway?"

"You did, remember?" Ace laughed. Millie's foul mood didn't ruin his fun at all. In fact, it seemed to somehow make the entire situation even more comical to him.

Nan stood next to the ditch, evaluating the situation. Jack looked at her helplessly, and Millie, face buried against her bent knees, burst into another round of sobbing. Kara patted Millie's shoulder, helpless to console her but adorable in her attempt.

"The mud is just too deep for Chubbs to walk out of," Jack said to Nan, who seemed to be the only other sane person in the bunch.

"We need a flat piece of wood or something to make a ramp for him to walk out of the hole," Nan told him. "Ace!"

Ace stopped laughing and took notice of the stern tone in Nan's voice. "What?" he gasped, once again trying to compose himself.

"Run back to Millie's house and look around the back yard for something we can stick down into the mud for Chubbs to walk on."

"Yes, ma'am!" Ace stood straight up and flapped a snappy salute at Nan before running back through the woods toward Millie's house.

"Now, let's get Chubbs calmed down before he hurts himself."

Jack looked grateful that Nan had shown up to take charge. Nan had to admit that she had a knack for organizing. Nan peeled off her shoes and socks and cautiously stepped into the mud next to Chubbs. She scratched between his ears like she had seen Kara do, and he slowly began to calm down.

"It's okay, Chubbsie," Kara crooned as she began to follow Nan into the mud.

"Stay by Millie!" Nan snapped. "That's all I need is for you to get hurt!" Kara stepped back toward a still crying Millie and sat next to her on the ground.

Before too long, Ace reappeared, lugging a long piece of plywood. He passed it down the hill to Nan and Jack. "I brought some rope, too," he said. "Maybe we can tie it around his belly to help pull him out."

"Thanks," Nan replied. She and Jack shoved the board down into the mud at Chubbs' feet and started to urge him to walk up onto the board. He refused to budge.

"Let's try the rope," Jack said. He turned to Ace, who tossed the coil of rope down to him. Jack and Nan managed to tie one end of the rope around the pig's belly and tossed the other end back to Ace. Ace pulled the rope taught and then wrapped it around his waist for extra leverage.

Jack pushed and Nan pulled on Chubbs until, finally, he decided to cooperate. He stepped up onto the board and, with Ace still pulling, lunged up from the mud and onto dry ground. Relieved, Nan and Jack followed and plopped down next to him. Chubbs shook himself like a dog, and Ace laughed as Jack and Nan were sprayed with mud. They laughed along with him, although Jack cut his laughter short, seemingly miffed at himself for laughing along with his stepbrother. "Let's go home and get cleaned up," said Jack.

"What about my treasure?" Millie exclaimed.

Nan lost it. "What is it with you and treasure hunting these days?" she asked. "Get real, there is no treasure. And what do you need it for, anyway? It's not like your parents won't buy you everything you want, you spoiled brat!"

"I am not spoiled!" Millie screamed at her. "I have to find a treasure, I MUST!" She stood up and stomped her feet.

Nan was used to Kara's tantrums but, on Millie, it looked ridiculous.

Even Ace seemed amazed. "Dude, relax!" he said.

Nan laughed at Ace calling Millie "Dude".

Millie was not amused. "I will NOT relax!" she yelled. "I'll yell all I want! We're about to lose our house and be homeless, and I'm going to have to live in a shelter somewhere with no new clothes, or shoes, or makeup, or anything! I have to find a treasure, I HAVE TO!" Millie collapsed onto the ground, sobbing once more, but this time with a hint of embarrassment in her tone.

Nan, Kara, Ace, and Jack all looked at Millie, astonished. They didn't quite know what to do or say. It was inconceivable that Millie, with her big, fancy house and constant flow of new clothes, could suddenly be poor. It just didn't make any sense.

Nan finally knelt beside Millie and put an arm around her shoulder. "It's okay," she said. "Why don't you tell us what happened? It can't be as bad as you think."

"Oh, it is. It is SO bad!" Millie exclaimed, sniffling and wiping tears from her eyes. She glanced up and suddenly realized that everyone was staring at her. She jumped to her feet self-consciously, nearly knocking Nan over. She stood and glared at Ace, almost daring him to make a snide remark. Ace wisely kept his mouth shut.

Millie turned her back to them and paced, first away from them, and then back. "I suppose I might as well tell you now," she said, finally. "You're going to find out anyway."

"Find out what?" Jack asked.

"That we're broke," Millie answered. "Our house is about to be foreclosed on if we don't come up with $30,000 by the end of the month!"

"What's a fork low?" Kara asked. The others were too stunned to speak.

"Foreclosed," Millie corrected. "It means the bank is going to take our house away from us, and we are going to be homeless!"

"What...how?" Nan stuttered. She had always thought Millie lived a charmed life, and she couldn't quite wrap her mind around the whole thing.

Millie's shoulders slumped forward. Her voice quieted as she took a heavy sigh.

"My parents owe too much money on their credit cards, and they can't pay the bills anymore," she told them. "Bill collectors call our house day and night, and my parents are fighting like crazy. I can't stand it anymore!" she moaned. "Oh, Nan, you're right. There is no treasure! This is all just stupid. My life is over!"

"Maybe Nan's wrong," Jack piped up, obviously desperate to help. "Maybe there is a treasure somewhere! I've heard stories about an old bank robbery back in the 1920s...the robbers stashed the money around town here somewhere, but then they were caught and thrown in jail."

"Yeah, I've heard that story, too!" Ace said, strangely drawn to give Millie some good news.

Nan grimaced. What was it about Millie that had people try to make her feel good all the time? Even Kara joined in by offering Millie her crown.

"My dad told me once that there's supposedly a huge stash of money that no one ever found," said Ace. "Maybe we could find it and save your house!"

"Really?" Millie asked, hopefully. She looked at Nan.

"What?" asked Nan, self-consciously.

"Do you think it's true?"

Nan could feel Millie's desire for some shred of hope pulling at her. There was no part of her that wanted to go looking for some supposed bag of money but she didn't feel like she had a choice "Well…I guess anything's possible," Nan offered.

"But how are we going to find it?" Ace asked. "I'm sure people have searched all over the place for it already. How do we even know where to begin?"

They all thought for a moment.

"Maybe we could go to the library and look at old newspapers or something," Jack said.

"Or, we could ask around and see if anyone remembers any of the old stories," Ace added.

"Would those people still be alive today?" Millie asked.

Nan tried to calculate in her head how old someone who lived in the 1920s would be now.

"Sure," Ace said. "They'd probably be in their 80s or 90s at least, but I bet there's someone around who could tell us something." He glanced at Millie's hopeful face and snickered.

"What's so funny?" Millie asked him, indignantly.

"You should really see yourself," he told her. The others looked at her and laughed as well. They weren't used to seeing her this way. In fact, after her recent admission, they were beginning to see her in a completely different light.

Millie ran her fingers over the mud that was now drying in clumps in her stringy blonde hair. She glared at them, her cheeks flushed with fire. Nan felt terrible.

Millic got up and started up the hill. "I'm going home…the home I *won't* be living in."

"Millie, wait!" Jack called after her. "Come back! It's okay, I promise!"

Nan looked at Ace and then followed after Millie and Jack. It was all so awkward.

"Come on, Millie!" Ace called. "I was just joking...I didn't mean anything by it. I'll help you find the treasure." He sighed loudly and started the trek up the hill.

Jack had caught up to Millie and put his hand on her shoulder.

"I don't need your pity, Jack," she snapped at him. "And I don't need your help, either! I'm not gonna go digging around some stupid library or talking to a bunch of old people about some treasure that probably never even existed! You've humiliated me enough with your stupid ideas!"

"Millie!" Jack's face fell and he looked like he was about to cry himself.

"Millie, no one is trying to humiliate you," Nan said. "We're sorry if we hurt your feelings." She looked over her shoulder at Ace.

"Uh, yeah!" he piped up. "I wasn't laughing at you, I was laughing with you…I, uh, just didn't realize you weren't laughing…"

Millie stopped and furrowed her brow, shaking her head at him.

Nan began to laugh. "That made no sense at all, Ace!"

Ace grinned sheepishly, and Jack laugh at him uneasily. Millie scrunched up her face. "Oh, I know you didn't mean it," she said finally. "I just don't know what to do anymore. I mean, I want to believe that there's a treasure out there somewhere, and that we can find it, but I've been so disappointed already. I just don't even want to think about it anymore!"

"It's okay, Millie," Jack told her. "We're your friends, and we're here to help you. No matter what you want to do, right guys?"

"Sure," Ace said.

Nan hesitated, not sure she wanted to completely commit to doing 'whatever Millie wanted' even if she was in a terrible situation.

Millie looked at her friends wistfully.

"Hey, what'd you guys do with my dad's metal detector?" Ace asked.

"Oh, I must have dropped it by the mud hole," Jack said. "I'll go get it." He began to jog back to where Chubbs had been stuck in the mud, when he suddenly stopped and looked around. "Chubbs!" he called. "Here, Chubbs!"

Nan suddenly realized she had left Kara. "Oh, no! Kara, where are you?!" she called.

There was no answer. Millie's predicament was forgotten for the moment as they all began to search for the missing members of their group. Ace stopped to retrieve the metal detector before climbing the next hill, calling for Chubbs and Kara along the way.

They heard Kara's thin voice calling through the trees. "I'm over here!"

"She must have wandered off the path," Jack said.

"Probably chasing after your stupid pig," Millie snipped at him.

"Kara, what are you doing?" Nan called. "You're supposed to stay with us!"

Nan pushed her way through a thicket of shrubbery and came across her sister trying to drag the pig away from a hole he was digging in the dirt.

"What is he doing?" Ace asked from behind her.

"Come on, Chubbs!" Kara, exasperated, pulled at Chubbs' collar, trying to get him to follow her.

"Does he always dig like this?" Ace asked Jack.

"Pigs like to rut around in the dirt," Jack replied, "but I've never seen him dig a hole like this." Chubbs pawed at the dry dirt with his cloven hoof, snuffling the dirt out of the hole with his snout.

"Maybe he just got a taste for dirt in that mud hole," Ace laughed. As he approached the pig, the metal detector, which

Jack had forgotten to turn off, began to beep loudly. Ace stopped and looked at the others.

Millie's face lit up. "The darn pig found something!" she exclaimed. "Hurry, let's dig!"

Jack grabbed the little shovel that he had stuck into his waistband earlier, and the others looked around for sticks to dig with. Ace held the metal detector over the ground, trying to pinpoint the exact area where it had gone off. "Right here!" he said finally. Jack began to dig in the spot Ace had indicated. "And here," he stated a moment later.

Millie began to dig there. Ace found spots for Kara, Nan, and himself to dig, too, and they all set to work. Meanwhile, Chubbs continued to dig in his own hole.

"Ah, it's just an old rusty nail," Nan said at last.

"Mine, too," Jack chimed in a moment later.

"I don't even know what mine is," Millie held up a chunk of rusty metal. "I knew it was too good to be true," she said, slumping down in defeat.

"Oh, look what Chubbs found!" Kara cried. The others ran to her, expecting to find some wonderful treasure, but it was only another rock.

"Look!" Kara beamed. "This one has writing on it, too!" She wiped the dirt from one smooth face of the stone, and handed it to Nan.

Jack put his hands on his hips and shook his head. "Well," he said, "if gold hasn't washed down from the hills, it looks like someone's rock collection did!"

Ace agreed. "I know, weird, right?"

Nan squinted at the barely legible words etched on the rock and read it.

– Have Faith –

"Okay, Jack, tell us what it means," Ace goaded.

Kara reached for her rock but Nan was still looking at it.

"Faith means believing in something even if you don't have proof that it exists," answered Jack.

"Faith is like hope," said Millie.

"Yeah, kind of," Nan said. She scrutinized the rock. "But it's different. Hope is just crossing your fingers. Faith is more…like, if you believe in something, it's somehow more possible than if you don't."

"Like finding buried treasure," Ace added. "If we have faith that it exists, we'll find it!"

There was a strange pause and Ace suddenly looked uncomfortable.

"I dunno," he shrugged. "I was just thinking out loud."

"But, it's not really the treasure we want," Jack said thoughtfully. "It's what we can do with the treasure once we find it."

"Yeah," Nan added, "maybe we need to have faith about the thing we're going to do with it. My mom always says that money is just a tool to make your dreams come true."

Millie was thinking, too. "Maybe it means if we have faith, then nothing can get in our way!" she exclaimed. "But how do you have faith if you don't really believe it can happen?"

"Just believe it," Kara said shrewdly.

They all looked at Kara, who always seemed to have something smart to say.

"And if you think about it, it kinda follows off the first rock," Ace said. "If you desire something, you have to want it so badly that you eventually believe it will happen." He paused and then added rather proudly, "Desire leads to faith."

"I wonder if it works in the opposite, too," Nan thought aloud.

"What do you mean?" Jack asked her.

"Well, if you constantly think that you are going to fail, then of course you will. If you don't have faith, then you can never accomplish anything."

"I guess that makes sense," Ace said thoughtfully.

"So, just have faith, Millie," Kara told her, placing her tiny hand into Millie's larger, dirtier one.

"Yeah, just have faith," Jack added, smiling at her. "If nothing else, have faith in us. We'll help you save your home."

Nan thought Jack was being overly optimistic and just a little too gallant. But Millie seemed to have that effect on Jack.

"Yeah," Ace patted Millie's shoulder. "I'll help, too."

Nan couldn't bring herself to join in the sudden "Support Millie" campaign but she smiled so she wouldn't look so obvious.

Millie glanced around and sighed. "Have faith," she repeated uncertainly. "I really hope it's that easy."

CHAPTER 4

# Mind Over Matter

While Millie ran inside her house to shower and change, the others rushed to bathe Chubbs with the hose in her back yard. "Please, don't tell my mom about this," Jack begged Ace. "She'll never let me take him out in the woods with me again if she thinks he's going to get into trouble like this."

"Ah, come on!" Ace joked. "I can't wait to tell my dad how funny you all looked stuck in the mud!"

"Please," Jack pleaded. He stopped scrubbing the dried mud from under Chubbs' belly long enough to give Ace a pained look. "I'll do anything!"

Ace rolled his eyes at Jack. "Don't worry, I'm no snitch," he stated. "Besides, it's probably only a matter of time before I do something that I won't want you to tell my dad about either."

Ace grinned at Nan. Jack sighed in relief. Nan knew he didn't need more trouble between his mother and his beloved pig.

Millie stepped through the sliding glass door onto the patio, fluffing her damp hair with her fingers. She wrinkled her nose in distaste at the site of Chubbs, who was wallowing in the attention he was receiving. "Are you almost done yet?" she asked him.

"Yup," Jack answered. "Nan, could you shut the water off, please?"

Nan turned the handle on the water spigot and stood up just in time to be splattered with water as Chubbs shook his entire body, head to toe.

"Let's go back to your house, then," Millie said. "My mother won't like seeing that animal on our lawn."

★ ★ ★ ★ ★

Mr. Emerson was filling a wheelbarrow with round river rocks from the back of his truck when they arrived at Jack and Ace's house. "What are you trouble makers up to today?" he asked them good-naturedly, as he began to push the wheelbarrow toward the back yard.

"Nothing," they chorused.

Mr. Emerson stopped and looked them over. "Yeah, sounds like nothing," he grinned. "Nothing always turns into something. You can count on it!"

Mr. Emerson was a much bigger version of Ace and appeared to have the same sense of humor. Although, being a policeman, Nan figured that he could probably be very serious, too, and good to have around.

"What are you gonna do with all those rocks?" Kara questioned Mr. Emerson. He stopped the wheelbarrow next to a round hole that he had dug in the back yard and turned to wink at Kara, just as Ace had done so many times.

"I thought we'd build a fire pit in the backyard this afternoon," Mr. Emerson answered. "After all, if we're going to have a hotdog roast, we'll need a place to roast 'em!"

"Me, too?!" Kara asked excitedly.

"You, too, Little Miss," Mr. Emerson said playfully.

"Awesome!" Ace exclaimed.

Nan wasn't a big hotdog lover, but it sounded like fun, and she realized it hadn't taken long at all for something to come out of nothing!

"Why don't you kids bring those rocks over here so I can start lining the fire pit?" Mr. Emerson said.

"Sure!"

Ace and Nan began to hand the rocks to him one at a time while Jack and Millie stood back and watched. Millie probably didn't want to get her hands dirty any more that day, and Jack was doing his best to appear bored at the idea of having a bonfire with his new stepfather.

Kara picked through the wheelbarrow, looking carefully over each rock. Nan admired her sister for her appreciation of simple pleasures, wishing her own mind would give up some of its constant chatter.

Mr. Emerson began at the center of the hole he'd dug and laid the rocks in a single spiraling layer, out from the center. "I'll just build this up," he told them as he started the second layer. "We wouldn't want to start a forest fire now, would we?"

He winked at Nan and, when he did, she recognized an old but very subtle feeling of safety. It somehow reminded her of her dad and she made a mental note to write about that in her journal later.

"Nan, Nan!" Kara suddenly exclaimed. "Look what I found!"

Nan looked over. Kara was holding up a rock. "It's another rock with writing on it!" she cried, excitedly. "Read it, read it!" she begged. Kara jumped up and down as well as she could considering the weight of the rock.

Nan took the rock from Kara and looked it over.

"I'm a magic rock finder! I find rocks everywhere!" said Kara.

Nan couldn't disagree. The fact that her sister had now found three rocks with writing on them was feeling a little unbelievable.

This latest rock was perfectly smooth, solid, and shaped almost like an egg. Tiny little specks of glassy sand glistened from underneath its surface. Nan tilted her head to get a better look and rotated the rock in her hand as she read the words delicately etched upon it. The others crowded around to see.

– Repeat Positive Thoughts –

"Well, I can certainly get behind that, can't you?" asked Mr. Emerson. Nan nodded. Her mom was constantly telling her to see the good in things.

Nan handed the rock to Mr. Emerson. "This is the third one she's found."

"What do you think, Dad?" Ace asked.

"I think Kara has a knack for finding special things," said Mr. Emerson, passing the rock back to Kara. She beamed.

"I also think that thoughts are very powerful things and we may as well think the positive ones," he added.

"What do you mean by 'powerful', Mr. Emerson?" Nan asked.

"Well, thoughts have the power to make things happen or set things in motion."

"I don't get what you're saying, Dad," said Ace.

"Okay," Mr. Emerson continued, "see if this helps. If I tell you to think of a lemon, what happens?"

"I get that funny feeling in my mouth," said Millie.

"Me, too," said Jack, "my mouth starts to water."

"That's right," said Mr. Emerson. "And what happens when you think about standing on a high diving board, ready to jump into a pool?"

"I feel a little scared," said Nan.

"Excited!" said Ace.

" Right. All those feelings came from just a thought. That's pretty powerful, wouldn't you agree?"

"I guess so," said Nan, thinking on it deeply.

"Do you think that it's true you can change your reality by changing your thoughts?" asked Jack.

"Mr. Professor here," Ace teased.

"Absolutely, Jack," answered Mr. Emerson. "The thoughts you put into your head become the thoughts you believe and act upon. Positive thoughts keep you going and negative ones hold you back."

"So," said Millie, "if we really want something, we have to tell ourselves that we can have it."

"Yes," said Mr. Emerson, "over and over again."

Kara jumped in. "Like *The Little Engine That Could*," she said. "I think I can, I think I can, I think I can."

"That's right, Kara," said Mr. Emerson, patting her back. "Good thinking!"

"How is that any different from just having faith?" Nan asked, thinking of the last rock.

"Give it a go. What do you think?" he asked.

Nan felt his genuine interest and responded. "Well, maybe instead of just believing something, we can actually change it inside of us," Nan ventured, looking to Mr. Emerson to back her up.

"Absolutely," he agreed. "Here's an example. It's like when I met your mom, Jack," he continued. "I thought she was probably out of my league. Now, if I had sat around telling myself that a woman like that would never go for a guy like me, she would never have known I was alive. Instead, I took one look at her and told myself, 'I am going to marry that woman.' I didn't make any excuses for why I couldn't, I just decided I would. I found a way to get someone to introduce us to each other, and the rest is history!"

"That is SO romantic!" Millie cooed.

Ace and Jack rolled their eyes at her at the same time.

Mr. Emerson paused. "You know," he said, "I have kind of a spooky story to tell you kids later that will show you just how powerful thoughts can be."

"Ah, tell us now!" Ace prodded his dad in the ribs.

"Patience, my son," Mr. Emerson replied. "Let's get this fire pit finished first."

* * * * *

The kids were stuffed full of hot dogs and chips but had plenty of room for dessert! Nan thought it was funny how you could be so full yet still have room for something sweet.

Mrs. Emerson passed around sticks and marshmallows for everyone and then lined up graham crackers on a plate. Millie helped with the S'mores by unwrapping the chocolate bars and laying them on top of each cracker.

Kara immediately set her marshmallow on fire, and began to wave it around frantically. Nan made a move to grab it from her but, in the short tussle, the fiery confection flew off Kara's stick and through the air, landing with a "squishy" plop against the side of a tree. Mr. Emerson jumped up to make sure nothing caught on fire and Ace doubled over in his chair, laughing. A moment later the lawn chair folded up on him, leaving him sprawled on the ground in front of the fire, causing everyone else to laugh. Ace's cheeks burned but his laughter seemed to bubble up above his embarrassment.

"Ha, ha!" he retorted. "You all got your laugh, now get back to your marshmallows!" At that, everyone only laughed harder. Ace stood up, unfolded his chair, and sat back down carefully.

"Why don't I roast another marshmallow for you, sweetie?" Mrs. Emerson kindly asked Kara, reaching for the roasting stick. Kara gladly handed it over, acting a little embarrassed at the commotion she had caused.

"How about that story, Dad?" Ace called across the fire.

"I hope it's not too scary," Mrs. Emerson warned him, casting a glance at Kara.

"Oh, it'll be okay," Mr. Emerson assured her. He reached for a graham cracker and put a S'more together for himself. The others looked at him impatiently while he leisurely munched away.

"Da-ad?" Ace prompted his father.

"Oh, you wanted to hear the story right now?" Mr. Emerson teased.

"Yes!" they all cried in unison.

"Okay," he said, finishing his tasty treat. He leaned forward in his seat, and the children leaned in as well. "This is the story of a man who thought himself to death."

"What?" Ace asked, dubiously.

"Shush, let him tell the story!" Millie reprimanded him.

Ace shrugged and let his father continue.

"A few years ago, I was called to investigate a strange death at a trucking company," Ace's father continued. "It was a hot day, and an employee at the company had climbed into the back of a refrigerated truck to cool off while he took his afternoon break. He left the door open so he could get back out, and then sat in a back corner of the truck and nodded off to sleep."

"What's a frigiated truck?" Kara asked through a mouthful of gooey marshmallow.

"A refrigerated truck," Mr. Emerson answered, "is a truck that has a cooling system in it so that cold stuff, like ice cream, can be hauled from one place to another without melting."

"Oh," Kara said, licking her fingers.

Mr. Emerson continued. "Well, another employee came along and thought that someone had left that door open accidentally, so he closed it."

Kara's eyes widened. "Did he wake up?" she asked.

"He did," Mr. Emerson told her. "The man woke up when he heard the sound of the door slamming shut. He jumped to his feet and yelled that he was in there, but the walls were so thick no one could hear him. He tried to open the door but it was locked from the outside."

"That sucks," Ace said.

"Ace, your language." Mrs. Emerson scolded him quietly.

"Sorry," Ace said sheepishly.

"What happened next?" Kara asked, enthralled with the story already. "Did he get out?"

"He died, remember?" Millie told her. "Remember, Mr. Emerson said this is the story about a man who thought himself to death?"

"But, how can you think yourself to death?" Jack asked. "Are you sure he didn't just freeze to death?"

Mr. Emerson raised a hand and motioned for them to settle down so he could continue. "Well, the man paced and yelled for a bit, trying to get someone's attention, but after a while he gave up. He was so cold he could hardly stand it anymore. He shivered and paced, and jumped up and down trying to keep his blood circulating. After a few hours, he started to believe that no one would ever come, and he would freeze to death in that truck."

"That's horrible!" Nan exclaimed. She couldn't think of anything worse than knowing you were going to die.

"After a while," Mr. Emerson continued. "The man got to thinking about his wife and kids. He had left that morning without telling them good-bye, because they were all asleep and he didn't want to bother them. He'd also had a fight the night before with one of his sons, and he didn't want his last words to him to be angry words."

"Oh, how sad," Mrs. Emerson said.

"So, the man felt in his pocket for the little log book that he carried with him at work, and he sat down to write a letter to his family."

"How could he see to write if the truck was closed so tight that no one could hear him yelling?" Jack asked in disbelief. Nan was also beginning to doubt that the story was really true.

"Good question, Jack," Mr. Emerson said. "He probably just turned on the little overhead light that is in the back of most refrigerator trucks. This was a couple of years ago, so of course I don't remember all of the details."

Jack seemed satisfied with this answer, and Mr. Emerson continued. "So anyway, he sat down to write a letter to his family."

"You said that already," Ace told him.

"No more interruptions!" Mr. Emerson scrunched his face up and pointed across the fire at Ace, who laughed back at him good-naturedly. They seemed to have a fun relationship.

"Anyway…" Mr. Emerson went on, "the man sat down and wrote out an apology to his family for getting himself locked up in the truck. He said he should have known better. He also told his son he was sorry for arguing with him. He told all of them how much he loved them."

Kara's eyes were as big as saucers as she listened intently to the story. Everyone leaned quietly forward, anxious to hear the end.

"After a while, the man gave up altogether and decided to write down what it was like to freeze to death. He figured that since no one had ever lived through it before, maybe his death could at least provide a service to society. He sat down once more with his pad of paper and turned to a new page. He wrote about how long he thought he'd been in there and about the changes that he was feeling in his body. He could feel his blood slowing, and his brain shutting down. After a while, he could write no more, so simply laid down and died."

"Oh, no!" Mrs. Emerson said, horrified. "Maybe this wasn't such a good story to tell the children."

"Wait, now," Mr. Emerson waved her off. "I haven't told the most important part."

"Are you sure it's okay?" his wife asked him, eyeing little Kara.

Mr. Emerson nodded and continued. "The next morning, a mechanic opened the back of the truck, preparing to climb inside and work on the cooling system, which had broken."

"Wait a minute!" Jack exclaimed. "Now I know you're just making this up. You just said the guy froze to death, but how could he if the cooling system was broken?!"

"Maybe the switch froze in the 'on' position," Nan piped up. She glared at Jack for once again interrupting the story.

"Ah, but Jack's right," Mr. Emerson conceded. "At least partially right, anyway. You see, and I'm not making this up, the truck *was* broken and the man did not freeze to death. It was 68 degrees inside the back of that delivery truck when the man's body was found." He stopped to allow this new bit of information to sink in.

"Well, what happened to him then?" Millie demanded.

"The man thought himself to death," Mr. Emerson answered her.

"What? How?!" Jack stammered. "That just doesn't make any sense. How could he think himself to death?"

Mr. Emerson began to explain. "After a lot of investigating, we finally pieced together what had happened. It was so hot outside, that when the man stepped into the truck, it made 68 degrees feel much cooler than it actually was. The man fell asleep and woke up disoriented, and then he panicked. He *thought* that the truck was working. He *knew* that there was no way anyone could survive for long locked up in one of those trucks. It never occurred to him that the refrigeration system wasn't working." Mr. Emerson paused. "Our thoughts are powerful things."

"That couldn't really happen, could it?" Jack asked incredulously. "I mean, there has to be some scientific explanation for the man's death other than he just *thought* himself to death. That's just silly!"

Nan felt a cold shiver up her spine as she considered it.

"Jack," Mrs. Emerson said, with a hint of a warning in her tone.

"There's just no telling what the human mind can achieve," Mr. Emerson shrugged. "What do you think, Millie?"

"I think it's totally freaky," Millie told him. Mr. Emerson laughed.

Suddenly, from out of the dark, came a blood curdling squeal, and they all jumped and screamed. They started laughing, though, when they realized that it was only Chubbs, probably wanting to be with everyone.

Nan made a mental note to write some of the things she wanted to use her thoughts to change in her journal, like thinking herself into a nice big house!

CHAPTER 5

# Looking for Answers

The next morning dawned bright and hot. It was so hot, in fact, that Nan was up and ready to head out of the building at the same time as her mother. Even Kara was ready to escape the oppressive heat that was already beginning to build inside their tiny apartment.

"Don't forget I have my accounting class tonight," Ms. Webster reminded her daughters, "so I'll be late again."

"Ugh, Mom!" Nan groaned. "Why do you waste your time on those stupid classes? It's not like you need accounting to be a waitress!"

"Oh, Nan," she sighed. "Education is never a waste. When you invest in yourself, it always pays off."

"Whatever," sassed Nan. She was tired of hearing her mother's thoughts on investing. She always seemed to have something to say about everything.

"Anyway," Ms. Webster continued, "tomorrow, I'm off all day. I thought maybe we'd take the bus downtown to the library."

"Oh, goody!" Kara exclaimed. "Can I get some books tomorrow?"

"Of course you can," Ms. Webster replied. "There's also a free movie showing in one of the conference rooms. I thought we'd pack a picnic lunch and go to the park afterward...make it a family day! What do you think?"

"Fine," Nan shrugged, nonchalantly.

Kara, on the other hand, jumped up and down with excitement. "Yay!" she cried.

"You girls try not to spend too much time out in the heat today without drinking lots of water," Ms. Webster warned them as they went their separate ways. "Mrs. Emerson said you could spend the day at her house in the air conditioning if you like."

"What about you?" Nan asked her mother.

"What about me?"

"Well, just look how far you have to walk, and you don't even have a water bottle," she pointed out. "You have to work all day and then go to school"

"I'll be okay," Ms. Webster replied, hugging her daughter. "For your information, I've got a bottle of water in my bag."

"Bye, Mommy!" Kara hugged her mom and skipped away.

"Wait up for Nan!" Ms. Webster called after her.

"You girls be careful and have fun today," she said to Nan, hugging her tight with one arm.

Nan ran to catch up with Kara. "Slow down!" Nan cried. "It's too hot to run!"

Kara stopped. "Do you think Mrs. Emerson will let Chubbs back in the house today since it's so hot?" she asked.

"Yeah, right!" Nan said. "I just hope Jack doesn't want to spend the entire day suffering outside with him!"

"I'm not hot," Kara said, wiping the sweat from her brow.

Nan scoffed. "I also hope Millie doesn't drag us all over the country looking for buried treasure."

Nan rang the doorbell when they reached the Emerson's.

"Good morning, girls," Mrs. Emerson said cheerfully, upon opening the door. "Come in and let's get you something to drink. You must be parched!"

You could always count on Jack's mom to give you something yummy to eat or drink, just-baked or freshly-squeezed!

"Can Chubbs come inside today?" Kara asked loudly. Nan shot her sister a killer look.

Mrs. Emerson shook her head. "I'm sorry, Kara, but Chubbs has gotten way too big to live in the house. But don't worry about him. Mr. Emerson built him a nice little shed to get out of the sun, and we're making sure he has lots of water."

"All right," Kara pouted.

Nan rolled her eyes behind Kara's back, but Mrs. Emerson merely gave her a gentle smile.

"You have such a kind heart, Kara," Mrs. Emerson told her. "Maybe you can go out with Jack later and help him spray Chubbs with the hose. He likes to roll around in the mud a bit when he's hot."

Kara perked up as Jack's mother handed a glass of lemonade to each of the girls.

"The boys are watching TV in the living room," Mrs. Emerson said, ushering them out of her kitchen.

Nan and Kara found Ace and Jack slouched at opposite ends of the sofa, each trying to pretend that the other didn't exist.

"Hey!" Ace brightened up.

Jack only slouched deeper into his seat and scowled.

Kara bounced onto the couch next to Ace and snuggled in to watch the TV.

"What's wrong with you?" Nan asked Jack.

"Nothing."

"He's mad because I'm not letting him watch his stupid morning news show," Ace said.

Jack sneered.

Just then the doorbell rang.

"Millie's here," announced Ace.

Jack jumped up, his mood obviously improved while Ace's darkened.

"Run, kiss your girlfriend!" Ace goaded.

Jack kicked Ace on his way to the door, careful to jump quickly out of Ace's reach.

"That wasn't very nice!" Kara scolded Jack.

"It's okay," Ace whispered to her. "I'll take care of him later when he least expects it."

Kara grinned.

Nan peered around the corner to see Mrs. Medlin breeze through the door in front of Millie and kick off her designer sandals.

"Oh my gosh!" exclaimed Mrs. Medlin. "It is SO hot out today!" She quickly went into the kitchen without even acknowledging the kids.

"Hi, Millie," Jack said.

"Jack," she answered nonchalantly, flipping her hair over her shoulder as she pranced proudly past him. Millie walked into the living room and tapped Kara's leg, indicating that she should scoot over and allow Millie to sit next to Ace. That was just the kind of thing Nan hated about Millie and she was glad Kara didn't budge.

Millie glared at Kara, then turned with a flounce and plopped down into an armchair. She got right to the point. "So, where should we dig today?"

"Oh, Millie, it's so hot today!" Nan groaned.

"You promised you would help me," Millie reminded her.

Nan gritted her teeth. She didn't want to go back on her word, but she also didn't want to die of heat stroke.

Ace backed Nan up. "It would be stupid to go digging around all over the place without finding out where there might be something buried," he said.

Millie folded her arms across her chest, chagrined. "Well, how are we supposed to figure that out?" she demanded.

Ace stood and walked to the bookcase. "My dad has some books on local history, maybe we'll find something there." He ran a finger over the book titles, but didn't find what he was looking for. He picked up a round alabaster bookend. "Wow, this is really heavy," he said, hefting the bookend like a hand weight.

"That's so pretty!" Kara exclaimed. She had followed closely behind Ace and reached for the bookend. He placed it carefully into her hands.

"It's really heavy," he warned her.

Kara carefully took the bookend and ran her fingers over its smooth, glossy surface. "Is this made of rock?" she asked. "I wish I could have this for my collection."

"We'll find you another rock even prettier than this one while we're hunting for Millie's treasure," Ace promised.

"Yeah, but will it have writing on it like this one?" Kara asked him. "All my other rocks have writing on them."

"Let me see that," Ace said as he reached for the bookend.

Nan jumped up to have a look. "Wow, Kara," she said, "you did it again!"

"Yep! I find all the rocks with writing on them!"

Ace read the inscription to himself.

"This is perfect," he laughed. "Even the rock says we should do some research before running all over the place without a clue about what we're looking for!"

Millie glared. "How do you figure that, Mr. Know-it-all?"

"It says it right here," replied Ace. He read the inscription out loud.

- Gather Knowledge -

"Come on, Millie," said Ace. "It makes sense. We have to be smart about this and get more information."

"And, what do you propose we do?" posed Millie.

"What about that story we were talking about with the bank robbery?" said Jack. "No one ever found the money they stole from the bank, remember? Let's look into that."

"You know," said Nan, "that story does sound a little more familiar now that you mention it again. Maybe I heard about it in school or something."

"Sure, we could look online and see if we can find something about it," Jack replied. He went to the desk in the dining room and turned on the computer.

"We're going to the lib'ary tomorrow," Kara piped up. "They have lotsa books there on stuff!"

"They have computers at the library, too," said Ace.

"Fine, then," Millie decided. "We're all going to the library tomorrow."

"Well..." Nan hesitated. She didn't really want everyone butting in on her day with her mother. "I guess I could ask my mom if you can go along."

"Even if your mom says no, we could always just meet you there," Millie said.

"Fine," said Nan. She could see that Millie was going to get her way no matter what Ms. Webster said. "I'll ask."

"Good," Millie told her. "We'll meet at your house in the morning."

★ ★ ★ ★ ★

The next morning, Ms. Webster led the way to the bus stop down the street. Millie walked at her side and chattered away, with Jack following like a puppy. Nan trudged alone behind them, lugging a picnic basket with lunch for six. Ace and Kara wandered along behind her.

Realizing that Nan was struggling, Jack dropped back and grabbed the heavy basket from Nan who smiled. Nan liked that Jack paid attention to other people, especially when it wasn't always Millie.

Before they reached the bus stop, Ace turned his back to the group and took Kara's hand. Nan slowed and looked back. "I have a present for you," Ace whispered, giving her a wink.

"Really?" Kara asked, looking up at Ace in awe. He slipped something into her hand and grinned. Kara looked up in disbelief. Nan could see that it was a broken piece of Jack's mother's alabaster bookend.

Kara gasped and looked at Ace with wide eyes. "You broke it!" she whispered sharply.

"Not me!" Ace informed her. "My moron stepbrother was screwing around, trying to show off last night and knocked it off the shelf. I saved this piece from the garbage. See, I even got you the piece with the writing on it." He pointed to the elegant lettering on the rock which was, indeed, completely intact.

"Oh, thank you!" Kara grinned from ear to ear and took Ace by the hand.

When they reached the others, Ms. Webster directed Kara into the only open seat, while the rest of them stood close together holding on to one pole near the middle of the bus.

"A lot of people going downtown today!" Ms. Webster said, making conversation. "Are you all looking for something special or just getting out of the neighborhood for the day?"

Jack opened his mouth as if to speak but Millie cut him off with an elbow to his ribs. "Oh, we're just bored with hanging out around the neighborhood," she answered nonchalantly.

"I see," said Ms. Webster. "Well, I hope you all can manage to keep yourselves entertained long enough for me to get my research done."

"Yes, ma'am," Ace replied politely. "We're just looking for some interesting books on local history and maybe we'll play around on the computers for a little bit, too."

No one had much to more say during the fifteen minutes it took to get downtown.

"Well, here we are!" Ms. Webster said when the bus came to the library stop. She grabbed Kara by the hand and herded them all off of the bus.

Millie dashed excitedly up the front steps of the massive building. "Let's go!" she called impatiently.

Nan groaned and rolled her eyes. She looked toward her mother who smiled.

"I'll be in the reference room," Ms. Webster said to Nan, taking the picnic basket from her. "I'll try not to take too long, but come get me if I don't find you by noon."

Nan nodded her head, drew a deep breath, and ran to catch up to the others. A blast of cool air met her as she stepped through the door that Ace held open for her.

"So, where to first?" Ace asked.

"Let's start with the Internet," Jack answered. "If you can't find it on the net, you can't find it anywhere!"

"Works for me," Millie said, leading the way toward a bank of computers at the back of the library.

The computer lab was almost full but, luckily, Jack was able to slip into a chair in front of the last available screen. The others gathered around him, each trying to peer over his shoulder as he brought up the Internet. He typed "Treasure" into the search box.

"Okay, let's see," Jack mumbled to himself as he clicked on the first link.

"Don't do that!" Ace exclaimed, poking his stepbrother in the back. "That page has nothing to do with what we're looking for!"

"How do you know?" Jack elbowed him back.

"Read the description, moron! You can't just go clicking on every single link or we'll be here all summer!"

"Shhh!" A crabby looking old man shushed them from the next computer.

"Sorry," Nan apologized.

"Would you just let him look?" Millie hissed at Ace. "Jack knows everything. Why should we listen to you?"

"I know how to find stuff on the Internet and I know you're never going to find anything that way!"

"You guys!" Nan tried to quiet them.

"Why are you even here?!" Jack snarled at Ace. "You are so ignorant, it's not like you'll be any help to us. Why can't you just stay home and stop tagging along after me?"

"I want him here!" Kara defended Ace. "And he's not iggorant!"

Ace turned to Jack. "I'm not ignorant just because I don't cram my head full of useless information like you do. I can find what we're looking for just as easily as you can!"

"Shhh!" The man at the next computer growled at them again.

"Come on, Kara." Ace took her by the arm and began to lead her away. "We're going to do this another way."

Millie stayed glued to Jack's side, while Nan looked helplessly back and forth between the two halves of her group. Her face flushed with embarrassment as she realized the man was still glaring at them, so she decided to follow her sister and Ace.

"Ace, slow down!" Kara cried as he dragged her across the library.

"Oh, sorry," Ace said. "Are you okay? Jack just makes me so mad!"

"She's fine," Nan answered for her sister. "So, what now?"

"Let's find a librarian."

"Can't we just look something up in the card catalog instead of bothering a librarian?" Nan asked. She hated to bother people if she didn't have to.

"We could," Ace told her, "but that would just take more time, and I am GOING to find something before Jack does.

Besides, that's what the librarians are here for. If we didn't give them something to do, they wouldn't have jobs, would they?"

"I guess not," Nan conceded.

"Beside, my dad always says 'Work smart, not hard,'" Ace said.

He approached a librarian who was putting books away. "Excuse me, ma'am. Do you know where we can find books on local history?"

Nan was impressed. Suddenly Ace seemed completely confident and in control of the situation.

The petite woman stepped down from the stool she was using and smiled kindly at them. Nan hadn't seen such a young librarian before.

"Of course," said the woman, "follow me."

Ace grinned at Nan triumphantly as they followed the librarian.

"We have an entire section of books on genealogy and local history right back here. What exactly are you looking for?"

"We're looking for treasure!" Kara piped up.

Nan shot her sister a warning look. "No, we're just doing research on a story we heard about a bank robbery back in the 1920s," she explained.

The librarian's face lit up. "I've heard that story, too!" she told them. "That's one of my grandmother's favorite stories from the old days. She actually lived across the street from the bank when the robbery took place."

"Really?" Nan asked.

"Cool!" Ace added.

"Here we go." The librarian pulled a book from the shelves and rapped her knuckles on its hard cover. "This is exactly what you need. This book will have the most comprehensive account of the bank robbery. I wish you could talk to my grandmother, though. She has some wonderful stories to tell about the 20s."

"Do you think we *could* talk to your grandma?" Ace inquired. "I mean, if it wouldn't be too much trouble. We wouldn't take too much of her time."

Nan was surprised at Ace's forwardness.

The librarian seemed equally surprised, but thoughtful. "You know," she said, "maybe you could." She smiled again. "Yes, you *should* go see my grandmother," she continued, decidedly. "She loves kids, and I know she would love the company. She would love to sit and tell you stories for an afternoon. It would make her day!"

"That would be awesome!" Ace replied.

Nan was impressed once again by how quickly Ace had managed to find exactly what they were looking for.

"Let me just grab a sheet of paper and write down the information."

The librarian walked toward a desk and Ace followed her, carrying the book. Kara glanced up at Nan who shrugged her shoulders and followed along, as well.

"My name is Samantha Douglas," the librarian told them, as she wrote. "Everyone just calls my grandmother Grandma Douglas. That's just how she is...Grandmother to all who will have her." Samantha smiled to herself. "You just be sure to call her Grandma Douglas and tell her I sent you. She'll be glad to see you."

Samantha tore the paper in half and handed her notes to Ace.

"Wow, thanks!" he told her.

"No problem," Samantha replied. "If anything, it makes me happy that you're going to spend some time with my grandmother. Now, be sure and come back to see me if you need anything else, okay?"

"Oh, we will," Nan said. "Thank you so much!"

"Have a good day now." Samantha walked away to return to her work.

Nan and Ace looked at each other and grinned.

"That was so cool!" Nan told him.

Ace agreed. "So let's go find Jack and rub it in!"

Nan and Kara laughed, and they headed back toward the computer lab. They found Millie sitting at the keyboard with Jack hovering behind her.

"Millie, just let me do it!" Jack said, wringing his hands.

"Back off, Jack!" Millie admonished. "Ace was right, you know so much, but you have no idea what to do with all that useless information…oh, I hate this stupid computer!"

"Jeez, Millie," sighed Jack.

"You guys almost done?" Ace interrupted with a self-satisfied grin on his face. "I think we found exactly what we need."

Millie spat out her words. "Well, I hope you found something because Jack is useless!"

Nan hated how Millie could turn on Jack so fast. Millie took him for granted and Nan felt protective.

"How am I supposed to get anything done with you shoving me out of the way?"

"Girls, girls…" Ace grinned at them.

"Stop calling me a girl!" Jack almost shouted and was met with a round of shushing from the other people in the library.

"Can we go outside and talk please?" Nan suggested.

"What's there to talk about? I got everything we need," Ace gloated, "so we even have time to go watch that movie before we meet Nan's mom.

CHAPTER 6

# Imagine That

Nan's mother pushed through the main doors of the library and stepped out into the heat carrying their lunch. Nan followed, holding Kara's hand, and then Jack and Ace tried to fit through the door at the same time. They scuffled for a few seconds before an irritated Millie shoved them from behind and nearly sent both boys sprawling to the ground as she pressed past them.

"Watch it!" Ace grumbled.

"Oh, grow up!" Millie said as she descended the steps to the street. "Both of you are so juvenile!"

Nan did not disagree this time.

"Are you all coming?" Ms. Webster called to them.

"Yes, ma'am!" Ace replied, kicking Jack in the shin before running to catch up with the girls. Nan couldn't understand why boys had to be, well, such boys!

Once the group had assembled, Ms. Webster directed them down the street to a nice little park bordering the river that ran through town.

"Don't get too close to the water!" Ms. Webster called out to Kara, who started running after a couple of squawking ducks. "Nan, help me spread the blanket over here under this tree."

Nan and Ace each grabbed a corner of the old, ragged quilt and spread it on the ground in the shade. Ms. Webster began to unpack the picnic basket. Kara, whose chase had been interrupted by the ducks splashing into the river, ran to join the others in the shade. She jumped onto the blanket on her knees, right next to Ace, but immediately jumped back up, howling and grabbing her knee.

"Kara, what happened?" Ms. Webster asked her in concern.

"Owie! Owie! Owie! Something bit my leg!" Tears ran down her face, and she collapsed against Ace.

Ms. Webster reached across the others and gathered Kara into her arms and onto her lap. "Let me see, sweetie." She managed to pull Kara's hands away from her knee so she could see the large, angry bruise that was already beginning to form.

"Ow, what did you fall on, baby?" Ms. Webster leaned forward to kiss her daughter's injured knee.

"I don't see anything," Ace stated, feeling around on the blanket where Kara had landed. "Oh, wait! There's a big rock under here!" He pulled the blanket back to reveal a jagged stone that stuck up out of the dirt. He tried to brush the rock away but it didn't budge.

"Dig it up!" Kara commanded, still crying but not as hard.

Ace grabbed a stick and began to dig at the dirt surrounding the rock. He wiggled it out of the ground and held it up triumphantly. "Ta-da!"

Nan smoothed the blanket out so Kara could sit back down and offered her a hand. Kara settled gently into her seat, sniffling with her lips puffed out in a sad pout. Ms. Webster began handing sandwiches around and opened a bag of chips.

Ace stood and wound his arm up, preparing to launch the offensive rock into the river.

"Wait!" Kara cried. "I wanna see it!"

"Kara, I really doubt that rock has any writing on it," Nan said, rolling her eyes.

"Seriously, Kara," Millie added, pulling her sandwich apart and taking out the cheese.

"Just let me see," urged Kara.

Ace shrugged and handed the rock to Kara. He sat back down and began tearing into his own sandwich, eating heartily.

Kara grabbed a napkin and began to rub the dirt off of the rock. "Oh my gosh!" she cried, grinning through her now-forgotten tears and holding the rock up for everyone to see.

"No way!" Jack exclaimed, reaching for it. Kara handed him the rock, still grinning.

"I don't believe it," Nan exclaimed. "You're lying!"

"What is it?" Ms. Webster asked.

"No way!" Jack repeated his earlier sentiments. "There *is* writing on it! Look!"

"What does it say?" Millie asked.

"This is beyond weird," said Ace, shaking his head.

Jack cleared his throat. "Okay, you guys ready for this?" He read the words aloud.

– Use Your Imagination –

"Let me see that," Nan demanded.

Jack passed the rock over to Nan. She turned it in her hand and shook her head. "I don't get it! Where are all of these rocks coming from? It's just too big of a coincidence. It's almost as if someone is putting them here for us to find!"

"I know!" Kara quipped. "I find them everywhere!"

"It's an interesting phenomenon, isn't it?" Ms. Webster added.

"What is?" Nan asked.

"That when something is in your consciousness, you start noticing that particular thing more and more. Maybe those rocks have been lying around all this time and you're finding them now because you're tuned into them. Or at least Kara is!"

The kids all stopped and thought for a moment.

"She believed it was possible!" said Jack.

"But it already had writing on it before she had the thought," countered Nan.

"Yes, but Ace would have just tossed the rock into the river. We wouldn't have given it another thought if Kara hadn't *imagined* that it could have writing on it. We would have overlooked something that was already there."

Ace asked, "Well, if we keep imagining something's out there but we don't seem to be finding it, what are we doing wrong?"

"We're obviously not looking hard enough," Millie said.

"You might be looking too hard," offered Ms. Webster.

"What do you mean?" asked Millie.

"Well, let's say you were looking for treasure," said Ms. Webster.

Nan looked at her mom, wondering if she had known all along what they were up to.

"If we think that the thing we call 'treasure' looks like a chest with gold in it, then that's all we'd be looking for," said Nan's mom. "We'd probably miss the treasure that comes in a different form."

Millie's eyes lit up in a way that reminded Nan of flashing dollar signs.

"So, maybe there *is* treasure right under our noses," said Millie, "and we just never noticed it because we were looking for the wrong thing!"

"Well, Millie," said Ms. Webster, "you have to remember that sometimes treasure is not even necessarily a 'thing.' Sometimes the greatest treasures overlooked are the people around you."

Nan wasn't sure Millie could understand that concept at all.

"I think I get it," Jack said. "If you have an idea about something without making it look a certain way, it helps things stand out so you can see them. Maybe they just blend in with the background until you decide you want them and then they suddenly pop out!"

"I like your thinking, Jack," Ms. Webster smiled. "And here's another way Kara's rock ties in with all of this. Imagination is like a workshop inside your mind. We come up with ideas and then things come into our lives to help make them happen... like people, books, rocks..."

"You couldn't just imagine 'anything' and have it suddenly appear," Nan stated, ever the cynic. "I mean, if you imagine you want a helicopter, it's probably not going to just magically appear in front of you."

"Yeah, what about that?" Millie asked, doubtfully.

"Probably not," Ms. Webster acknowledged. "You won't find everything you imagine just lying about or falling into your lap. It takes some effort on your part."

The children looked puzzled, so she continued her explanation. "Maybe the thing you want won't appear out of nowhere, but the things you *need* along the way to *getting* that one big thing will start to appear. And then it's up to you to take those opportunities and run with them. Maybe those opportunities were there all along but you didn't see them because it hadn't occurred to you to look for them. Really, the only limitation is in your own mind. 'If you can think it, you can do it.' "

Kara bounced up and down. "I think I can, I think I can, I think I can."

"If you can think it, you can do it," Millie murmured to herself. She stuck her half-eaten sandwich back into its bag and leaned back on her elbows. The others continued to eat in silence, all rather thoughtful.

When they had finally finished eating they helped Nan's mother pick up the garbage and throw it into a nearby bin. Ms. Webster settled back onto the blanket with a book and began to read while the others walked down to the river's edge.

Despite her injured knee, Kara grinned from ear to ear as she admired the two new rocks in her hands.

Ace picked up another rock from beside the water and was about to throw it out into the river when he suddenly stopped himself. "So now I gotta look at every single rock I pick up to make sure it doesn't have any writing on it?" he asked, grinning playfully at Kara. He looked at the rock. "Nope, no writing," he told her. "It's safe to toss." Ace skipped the stone across the top of the still river, and they all watched it jump…one, two, three times.

"Wow, how do you do that?" Kara asked him in awe.

Ace showed Kara how to pick just the right size and shape of rock and began to tutor her on rock skipping. The other three sat back in the grass and watched.

"So, what opportunities for treasure have we overlooked?" Millie asked, anxious to discuss the one and only topic that currently held her interest.

"Oh, Millie…" Nan groaned. "Can't we just enjoy the day without worrying about treasure? I think we made a good start today. I mean, we found a book with tons of info on the 1920s, and we have an old lady we can go visit to get more information. Maybe that will be all we need."

Jack, who had brought the book along with him, flipped through it looking for the story about the bank robbery. "Here we go," he said, finally, poking a finger at the page.

Millie grabbed the book from him and began to read.

The two of them began to pore over the book while Nan leaned back in the grass to watch Ace and her sister. Ace really was kind of cute.

## CHAPTER 7

# Making Plans

"I'm so proud of you kids, taking the time to visit some of our senior citizens," Mrs. Emerson said the next morning when she dropped the five kids off at the Living Oaks Assisted Living Center. "I know that there are a lot of elderly people who don't get very many visitors. I'm sure they'll be so happy to have you! Really kids, I'm just so proud of you."

Nan felt a little guilty about letting Jack's mother heap praise on them for their selfless act, knowing all along that they had an ulterior motive for visiting Mrs. Douglas. She glanced at Millie who did not appear to hold any similar reservations. It was just like her to soak up the attention.

"We just thought it would be nice to do something useful over our summer vacation," Millie told Mrs. Emerson. "After all, life isn't all fun and games, is it?"

"So true," Jack's mother agreed.

Ace glanced at Nan before stepping out of the van. Nan was selfishly happy that he was getting a real taste of who Millie was.

"Well, have fun, and be good," said Mr. Emerson. "I'll be back after I run some errands."

Millie walked briskly into the building but stopped short just inside the door. "Ew," she whispered loudly, "it smells like old people in here."

Nan could swear that the nurse sitting at the front desk gave Millie a dirty look. "Can I help you?" she asked.

Nan pushed past Millie and made her way to the desk. "Yes, please," she replied. "We're here to visit Mrs. Douglas."

The nurse's stern frown seemed to soften a bit. "Oh, yes," she said to Nan. "You're the ones Samantha called about. She will be happy to see you."

"Thank you," Nan smiled shyly, then turned to glare at Millie who was still pinching her nose in disgust.

The nurse gave Nan directions to Grandma Douglas's room and buzzed them in. They walked tentatively down the sterile hall. Jack and Nan seemed to avoid making eye contact with any of the people they passed, while Millie made no effort to hide her disdain. Kara, of course, smiled and grinned at everyone who glanced her way.

"Old people give me the creeps," Millie said.

"You'll be old, too, some day," Ace told her.

He nodded politely to an elderly man who was slowly making his way down the hall with the aid of a walker. "Hi there," Ace said cheerfully. Then turning to Millie, he scolded, "Have a little respect!"

Nan felt horrible. She did not want to admit that she, herself, was somewhat afraid of old people. Some of them stared off into space with vacant eyes, while others smiled, seemingly hopeful that the children would stop and talk to them. One feisty old woman was arguing with a nurse, waving her away impatiently. "I think I can manage to make it to the day room without your help!" she snapped.

"Oh, I'll never be like them," Millie stated.

"Shut up, Millie!" Nan snapped. The others looked at her in astonishment. Nan mumbled, "Can we just get this over with already?"

"Here it is," Jack said finally, reading Mrs. Douglas's name over the room number by her door. "Should we knock?"

"Of course we should knock, you idiot," Ace told him. "What is with you people today?" He reached forward and rapped on the door.

A thin, sweet voice sang to them from the other side. "Come in!"

They glanced at each other hesitantly for a moment before Kara finally ducked in between the older children and pushed the door open. Mrs. Douglas was sitting in an old wooden rocking chair by the window, knitting something blue and green.

"Well, who do we have here?" Mrs. Douglas asked. "What a wonderful treat!"

"My name is Kara. We saw Samantha at the lib'ary and she said we should come visit you."

"Well, how sweet of her! Please, do come in. Who else do you have with you today, Kara?"

Kara was immediately drawn to the sweet old lady and sat right down on a delicate little stool at her feet. "This is my sister, Nan," she pointed. "And that's Ace, and Jack, and Millie."

"So nice to meet you all," Mrs. Douglas said, smiling at them. "Would you like a piece of hard candy?" She reached for a crystal dish that sat at her side.

"Okay!" Kara answered brightly.

"No thanks," Nan answered. Mrs. Douglas was just a normal person!

"I'll have one," Millie said, greedily. She took a handful, giving one piece each to Ace and Jack.

"Well, have a seat," Mrs. Douglas told them. "There aren't many chairs in here but you may grab a cushion out of the closet and settle in on the rug here by Kara."

Nan went to the closet and opened the doors. The small space was stacked full of stuff in wicker baskets and old hat boxes. She grabbed a couple of cushions out of a large container on the bottom and brought them to the others.

Once they were settled in a semicircle in front of Mrs. Douglas, Nan looked around. Trinkets and pictures adorned the entire room, and there seemed to be a beautiful lace doily under each and every knickknack. Not a speck of dirt showed on any gleaming surface in the room. It would have been impossible to find a more neat and orderly space in the entire world.

"What have you there?" Mrs. Douglas asked Jack, indicating the library book he had brought along with him.

"Oh...umm..." Jack stuttered.

"That's a book on local history," Ace broke in. "We were wondering if you could tell us about a bank robbery that took place in the 1920s. Your granddaughter told us that you lived near the bank."

"Oh, I did, indeed!" Mrs. Douglas replied. "Those were some hard times back then. The Depression had hit everyone hard, and crime was rampant. Some people were just trying to make ends meet any way they could, I guess. Not that I condone that kind of behavior, of course..." She trailed off, her eyes glazing over as she slowly rocked back and forth, perhaps recalling those hard times.

"Do you know where they might have hidden the money?" Millie asked bluntly. Nan elbowed her in the ribs but Millie ignored her and awaited a reply.

"Ah, treasure seekers, are you?" Mrs. Douglas winked at Millie. "You're not the first to come calling! But, I am sorry to say, that old legend about the bank robbers' buried treasure is just that...nothing but a legend."

"Oh no!" Millie cried out in disbelief.

Mrs. Douglas shook her head sadly. "Yes dear, nothing more than a rumor. I don't know how that story got started or even how it has lasted until today, but there never was any treasure. Those poor boys went in to rob that bank, not realizing that there wasn't any money left to steal. They got away with some change and that's about it...went to jail for stealing less than $10, those two did."

"Wow," Ace said.

The others were speechless. After all of this work to find out where the treasure might be, their plans were thwarted. Millie looked as though she might burst into tears.

"Why wasn't there any money?" Kara asked.

"Well, dear, there had been a run on the bank and any money to be had was long gone. My own father didn't make it in time to get his money out and he lost his entire life savings when the bank folded. Those were some really hard times."

"Mrs. Douglas...what's a run on the bank?" Ace asked.

"Oh, call me Grandma Douglas. Everyone does. A run on a bank is when everyone decides they want to get their money out in cash at the same time but the bank doesn't have enough money to give it to them. It happened everywhere during the Depression." She sat back and smiled and then began to tell the children what it was like growing up in the Great Depression.

Nan liked Grandma Douglas. She was warm and kind and spoke to them like they were adults. Nan hadn't spent much time with older people and it occurred to her that she might like to do it more.

Millie, on the other hand, did not look the least bit interested in what Mrs. Douglas had to say. Nan could tell that Millie was trying to give her the message that she wanted to leave but she pretended not to understand. Millie cleared her throat loudly in an attempt to get Jack's attention. She got Mrs. Douglas's' attention instead.

"There's a water fountain just down the hall," Mrs. Douglas offered.

Millie glanced at the floor, a little embarrassed. "Um…no, I'm okay," she said.

Mrs. Douglas continued talking and, before long, everyone but Millie was caught up in her tales of life long ago.

Kara sat listening…thoughtfully playing with her new favorite rock, which she had brought with her, tucked in her pocket. She felt its smooth edge and held it up in a stream of light that came in through the blinds.

A sparkle caught Mrs. Douglas's eye. "What do you have there, Kara?"

Kara smiled and proudly held up her prized possession. "This is my most favoritest rock in my whole rock collection!" she answered. "Here, look."

Mrs. Douglas took the rock from Kara's hand and looked it over. "Ah, yes. It is quite special. I like the inscription."

"All my rocks have words on them," Kara explained proudly.

"Hmmm." Mrs. Douglas held up the rock and looked at it again before returning it to Kara. She reached for her cane beside her chair and struggled to stand. Ace jumped up to take her arm.

"I think I might have something for you, dear."

"Really?" Kara's eyes shone with anticipation.

"Oh, yes."

Mrs. Douglas opened a drawer full of neatly arranged trinkets. "Let me see…ah, here it is." She turned back toward her chair with something small clutched in her hand. Kara's eyes were filled with anticipation as she waited patiently. Mrs. Douglas stretched out her arm and opened her fingers for Kara to see.

Kara gasped. "Oh boy! That's pretty!"

The others leaned forward to peer at a gleaming jade stone.

"And, what do you think of this?" Mrs. Douglas whispered to Kara as she turned the rock over in her palm to reveal the inscription on its back.

Kara's eyes widened even more. "What does it say?" she whispered loudly.

Mrs. Douglas read the words.

– Build Practical Plans –

"What's that mean?" Kara asked.

"Well, Kara, I've always used this paperweight as a reminder to make plans first, before getting started on anything," Mrs. Douglas answered.

"It's beautiful. May I see?" Nan asked, reaching for the rock. She held it under a lamp and read the words to herself before passing it into Jack's open hand. Jack handed the rock to Millie who glanced at it before tossing it carelessly to Ace.

"My dad says that people don't plan to fail," offered Ace, "they fail to plan." He smirked and looked pointedly at Jack who glared back at him. Nan grimaced uncomfortably as Ace seemed to one-up Jack once again.

"I would agree with that," said Mrs. Douglas, then added, "I would also say that your plans need to be practical and workable."

She held up her knitting. "If I didn't start with a good plan, this hat might end up looking more like a Christmas stocking! Now wouldn't that be silly?"

Kara giggled.

Jack saw his chance to join in the conversation. "You need organized planning if you want to make something happen," he said, "and you have to come up with a plan that makes sense and that you can actually stick with."

"That's right, Jack," said Mrs. Douglas.

"So, you shouldn't go running around looking for something without even knowing for sure if it exists, right?" Nan added, glancing over at Millie who had stopped listening and was staring off into space. Nan was hoping that the one person who needed advice the most about being practical was paying attention.

"Ah, now you're getting there," Mrs. Douglas nodded. "You can't win without a good plan. Mind you, having a plan doesn't guarantee success. You have to be willing to correct and continue as you go along."

"That makes sense," Jack replied.

"What I'm really trying to tell you," Mrs. Douglas said knowingly, "is that, even if you were to go looking for treasure with a plan, and even if you discovered that the treasure never existed in the first place, it doesn't mean that you can't keep looking for treasure. Right, Millie?"

Millie jerked her head up at the sound of her name. "Um, yeah, sure," she mumbled without really knowing what she was agreeing to.

"We just need a new plan!" Kara exclaimed, excitedly.

"It's like my dad always says," Ace added. " 'A quitter never wins and a winner never quits.' "

Mrs. Douglas added one more little distinction. "Exactly, but sometimes a quitter wins if he realizes his plan isn't working."

"Your dad really likes stupid clichés, doesn't he?" Jack asked.

Ace punched Jack in the arm. "Shut up, jerk."

Mrs. Emerson and a nurse stepped through the door just in time to catch Ace in the act. "Ace!" she exclaimed.

"Sorry," Ace mumbled, looking down at the floor.

Jack smiled, but Nan wasn't sure either of them should be too proud of themselves.

"I hope you aren't letting these kids wear you out too much," the nurse inserted.

"Oh, don't be silly," Mrs. Douglas rebuked, good-naturedly. "Certain kinds of tired are good for the soul. I hate to think of how boring life would be if I never let anyone wear me out!"

"Come on kids," Mrs. Emerson said, "it's time to go!"

"Aw, do we have to?" pleaded Kara.

"I'm afraid so."

Mrs. Douglas gave Kara a little squeeze. "You can come visit me again anytime you like, Kara."

Kara's face lit up. "Can we, Nan? Do you think mommy will let us?"

"Sure," Nan replied. "I would like to visit you again sometime, too."

"Me, too," Ace told her. "Your stories are really cool."

"Well, I'll tell you more stories than you can stand, young man," Mrs. Douglas assured him.

Ace grinned and followed his stepmother into the hall.

"I hope you boys weren't roughhousing the entire time you were here," Mrs. Emerson scolded. "You should know better than that."

"Yes, ma'am," Ace replied.

Ace was always so polite. Nan was sure Mrs. Emerson couldn't stay mad at him for long.

"Did you enjoy your visit?" Mrs. Emerson asked.

"Oh, yes!" said Kara, who began to chatter away happily, recounting the visit with Grandma Douglas.

⋆ ⋆ ⋆ ⋆ ⋆

"Well, that was a complete waste of time," Millie complained once they were back at Jack's house. She plopped down into a lawn chair.

"I don't think so," Nan contradicted. "I actually enjoyed it."

"Me, too," Ace agreed. "It reminds me of when I used to sit and listen to my grandma's old stories before she died. Don't you think it's interesting to hear what life was like a long time ago?"

"Who cares what life was like a hundred years ago?" Millie whined. "I care about life right now, and I need that treasure. It's not fair!"

"We can still look for treasure some other place," Jack said. "Like Grandma Douglas said, we just need a new plan. Pretty amazing how she pulled that rock out, huh?"

Jack let Chubbs out of his pen. The pig ran to the cool shade of a large tree and began to scratch his back against a root that was sticking up from the ground. Kara giggled and ran down to watch.

"Yeah," Ace agreed, "we just need a more practical plan this time, not some crazy buried treasure scheme, something that could actually work."

"Whatever," Millie grunted.

"I guess we could just give up," Nan stated, hopefully. She was tired of the whole project anyway.

Millie sat up, alarmed. "No, I don't want to give up!" she cried. "We have to do something!"

"Maybe we need to write something down," Nan said. "I think once we have something in writing it'll be easier to stay on track. That would be a good first step to turning our ideas into reality."

"That's not a bad idea," Jack agreed. "My mother is always saying 'see it, say it, write it down.' She says it helps people accomplish their goals, so maybe it could help us, too."

Ace jumped up, looking glad he had an excuse to do something. "I'll go grab some paper."

"We could try the metal detector again," Jack suggested when Ace returned. Nan took the note pad from Ace and began to write.

"Yeah, but we don't want to just run all over the place with it," Ace replied. "We should find good places where people lose things easily, like the beach."

"That's a good one," said Nan, and wrote it down.

"What about garage sales?" asked Jack. "I've heard of people finding stuff cheap and reselling it for tons of money."

"Oh, yeah!" Ace perked up. "My dad always watches this antique show where people bring stuff they found in their attic and find out how much it's worth. The other day, this lady found out she had a teapot worth $100,000!"

Millie jumped out of her chair. "A hundred thousand dollars? Seriously?"

"Seriously," Ace confirmed.

"Add that to the list," Millie ordered Nan.

"There's also the flea market at the Broad Street Fair Grounds," said Ace.

"Well, our list is starting to look pretty good," Nan said as she wrote. "But it's not really what I would call a 'plan'. Why don't we look at our options, figure out which ones are best and then write them down in the order we want to try them?"

"We also need to make a list of all of the tools we need and figure out how we're going to get to the places we want to go," Ace added.

"Let's also set a deadline," said Jack. "I work harder at my homework when I have a deadline I have to meet. If I have too much time to turn something in, sometimes I mess around and don't get it done 'til the last minute, and then it's not as good as I want it to be."

"You?" Ace asked in mock horror. "Are you trying to tell me that the amazing Jack Metter doesn't always do everything according to plan?"

"Shut up, you moron." Jack turned back to Nan. "I guess we should try to do it by the end of the summer for sure, since it'll be hard to go treasure hunting after school starts again."

"Does that work for you, Millie?" asked Nan, with a little bit of sarcasm.

Millie made a face at Nan. "Yes," she said, emphatically.

Nan finally gave in. "Well, Millie," she said, "now that we have a plan in place and a deadline set, I guess it's time to stop sitting around *imagining* your treasure and get to work finding it!"

CHAPTER 8

# Rummaging Around

"Kara, would you *please* stop blowing bubbles in your milk?!"

"But it's the way fish talk. I'm fish talking!" said Kara.

Nan grabbed the straw from Kara's cup. She was feeling cranky, despite the fact that their mom was treating them with cinnamon rolls.

Ms. Webster tried to do something special for them on the mornings when she went in to work late, even if it meant simply cracking open a roll of grocery store pastries or drinking instant hot chocolate with her and Kara.

Ms. Webster pulled the baking sheet out of the oven and tossed it onto the counter top with a clatter. "You have *got* to be kidding me!" she spattered.

Nan turned to her mother who was standing over the pan of pastry dough.

Kara stopped blowing bubbles in her milk just long enough to question her mother. "Whatsa matter?" she asked.

Ms. Webster shook her head in frustration and stuck her hand into the oven. "It's not even hot!" she exclaimed. "I can't believe this. If it's not one thing, it's another. This is absolutely ridiculous.

Oh, when I buy this building, this kind of thing won't happen every other day!"

"Oh, Mom!" Nan snapped. "Would you just give up on buying this stupid building already? It's never going to happen. You and Millie with your stupid ideas, running around looking for treasure and talking about buying an entire apartment building. Jeez!"

Nan's mother stopped what she was doing and looked at her older daughter, shaking her head sadly. "Well, I guess you are entitled to your own opinion, Miss Cranky Pants," she replied. "But, just so you know, people who make all of their decisions based solely on the opinions of others are generally failures. So, pardon me if I choose to keep dreaming about something that I know for a fact can happen if I just stick to my plan and don't give up."

Nan rolled her eyes and went back to her juice. She slouched down into her chair, trying to appear as small as possible. She felt badly for snapping at her mom, but not quite bad enough to apologize.

Ms. Webster changed the subject. "Alright, then. Why don't I just run this pan next door to Mrs. Thompson and see if she has room in her oven for them? Would you care to join me, Kara?"

"Yippee!" Kara jumped from her chair, dumping her milk across the table in the process.

"Oh, Kara," Ms. Webster groaned.

"Go on," Nan told her, wanting to make peace with her mother. "I'll clean it up."

"Thanks, Nannie."

Mrs. Thompson was a widow who lived in the apartment complex and made it her business to know everyone else's business. She was nice enough, though, and often looked in on the girls when Ms. Webster was working. Nan's attitude softened. She was actually always there to lend a hand whenever anyone needed it.

Nan quickly wiped up the spilled milk and looked up in surprise when her mother and sister reappeared within a couple of minutes. "That was fast."

"Look what Mrs. Thompson gave us!" Kara said as she carefully placed a covered basket on the kitchen table. Nan lifted a corner of the clean towel from the top of the basket and found a plate full of freshly baked, homemade cinnamon rolls. A heavenly aroma of sweet and spice wafted from the basket. Her eyes opened wide.

"Now, is that talent, or what?" Ms. Webster laughed. "I left with a pan of half-baked, canned cinnamon rolls and returned with a masterpiece!"

Nan reached for a huge, fluffy pastry that was still warm from the oven and gooey with frosting. "Mmmm," she murmured, happily taking a long, slow bite. "Mrs. Thompson's rolls are the best!"

Ms. Webster reached for a roll for herself. "She is such a sweet old lady. Wouldn't you know? Mrs. Thompson just happened to make these early this morning! She's going to finish baking those other rolls and give them to the delinquents in 210. I guess their mother has been gone for a few days on a job, and the oldest has his hands full with the younger ones. I am so glad I don't have to work the kind of hours that woman puts in. It's no wonder those boys are so difficult."

Nan shrugged, too busy eating to care about the five rowdy boys that lived down the hall. She and Kara tried to avoid them whenever possible, as they always seemed to be up to no good.

"So, what are you girls up to today?" Ms. Webster finally asked, after polishing off two rolls in silence. She took a sip of her strong, black coffee.

"We're going treasure hunting!" Kara piped up.

"I wouldn't really call it treasure hunting," Nan corrected her. "We're going to walk around some of the rummage sales in the neighborhood and see if we can find anything cool to buy."

"Oh, that sounds like fun. I haven't been to a rummage sale in I don't know how long!" Ms. Webster glanced at her watch. "Oh my goodness! I'd better get going."

"We should too," Nan replied. "Millie wants to get to the sales right when they started. She and Jack mapped out the entire neighborhood and dug through the classified ads to plan out the best times to get to each place. She's so bossy!"

"She sounds a lot like her mother!" laughed Nan's mom.

* * * * *

Millie was impatiently watching Jack talk to Chubbs in his pen when Nan and Kara arrived at the Emerson house.

"You act like that thing can understand what you're saying," she said in disgust.

"How do you know he can't?" Ace called from the patio where he was balancing a soccer ball on his head. "Pigs understand pigs."

"Ha, ha!" Jack replied testily.

Clearly, nothing much had changed overnight! She wondered if they would always be this way with each other.

"I feel so bad for him cooped up in this pen by himself," said Jack. "He hasn't been out running around with us in days!"

"Let's take him with us today." Nan suggested. She desperately wanted something to make Jack happy.

Jack hesitated. "I don't know…"

"No way!" Millie protested. "We do not have time to drag that stupid thing along with us today! We have to stick to our plan!"

"Oh, let him come," Ace said, catching the ball as it rolled off his head. "If nothing else, that stupid pig does provide some comic relief. I can't wait to see what kind of trouble he gets into today!"

"That's exactly what I'm worried about!" Millie said in her bossiest tone. "We don't have time to pull him out of the mud today!"

"What mud?" Nan asked, more than happy to oppose Millie. "There hasn't been a drop of rain in over a week and the ground is hard as a rock. I say we take him."

"Me, too!" Kara agreed.

"Then it's settled," Ace told Millie decisively. "The pig comes."

"Fine, but keep him away from me!" said Millie.

Ace grinned at Nan, and Jack opened the door to Chubbs' pen to free him. The gigantic potbellied pig trotted along after his master as docilely as any well-trained dog.

"What could possibly go wrong?" Ace laughed, nudging Nan.

"Oh, stop it," she said, laughing.

"I actually don't mind the pig that much, but don't tell Jack," confided Ace. "It's too much fun to tease him about it!"

Even though she didn't like keeping secrets, Nan somehow felt better about Ace and Jack, knowing how Ace really felt about Chubbs.

When they reached their first rummage sale, the group descended on the cluttered yard and began to pick through piles of junk with enthusiasm. The homeowner watched Chubbs with apprehension but the pig behaved perfectly, happily following Jack around the yard.

"You see anything?" Ace asked Nan after a few minutes.

"Nope, mostly clothes, and dishes, and other junk. I say we move on."

"Jack! Millie!" Ace called. "Let's go!"

"This could be harder than I thought," Jack said.

"Gee, ya think?" Ace rolled his eyes. "What did you think, we were just going to walk right up and find some priceless painting in the middle of that old lady's junk?"

"That would have been nice," Nan sighed.

They continued on, visiting one yard sale after another, and digging through more junk than Nan realized could exist.

"Why don't these people just throw this stuff in the garbage?" Millie asked after yet another disappointing sale.

"Maybe they need the money," Nan answered.

"Or," Ace added, "maybe they're just trying to recycle and keep their old junk out of the landfill."

"Whatever," Millie replied. "This stuff is just gross."

"What do you do with your old stuff?" Jack asked.

"I don't know," Millie shrugged. "But we sure don't stand around our yard begging our neighbors to buy it off of us!"

Nan pictured Millie throwing her practically new designer shoes into the garbage because they were scuffed, and felt sick to her stomach. Her own clothes were always packed away in boxes under her bed until Kara could grow into them. And even once Kara was finished with the hand-me-downs, her mother donated them to charity. Nan couldn't imagine just throwing away perfectly usable clothing and other stuff simply because she was too lazy to put them to good use elsewhere.

"Chubbs, get back here!" Jack called, running after his pig, who suddenly seemed overly excited to reach the next rummage sale.

"Chubbsie!" Kara cried, trying to keep up with Jack. Nan and Ace looked at one another and began to run as well.

"I told you so!" Millie called after them, strolling along at a leisurely pace.

"Chubbs! No!" Jack screamed, but he was too late.

The huge pig ran underneath a low table full of clothing. His back caught on the table and he dragged it several feet before tipping it over. The clothing fell into a huge pile on top of Chubbs.

He emerged with a long, purple scarf across his back that clung to him like socks with static electricity.

The young woman holding the sale turned and watched in astonishment as Chubbs leapt through the air and tried to grab a pink straw hat between his teeth. The hat slipped onto his head, and Chubbs began to run circles around the yard, trying to get the hat off of his head.

Ace was laughing so hard he had to sit down on the ground. "He looks like a gigantic ballerina!"

Nan stood in appalled silence, watching as Chubbs trampled through a pile of shoes, scattering them across the yard as well. Jack and Kara chased the pig, while Millie walked past as if she didn't know any of them.

Nan glanced at the woman who was holding the sale, fully expecting her to start screaming at them. But, after a few moments of confusion, she began to laugh along with Ace.

Finally, Jack managed to snatch the straw hat from Chubbs' head but the pig grabbed it out of his hands, coming to a complete stop and chomping down on the hat in his mouth.

"Oh my gosh!" Jack exclaimed, near tears. "I am so sorry!"

"We'll pay for that hat," Nan added. "I'm so sorry Chubbs wrecked everything!"

Millie had already walked down the block, obviously embarrassed. A boy on a tricycle had also stopped to see what was going on. Nan gave Ace a shove and told him to get up.

"Oh my goodness, it's okay," the young lady said with a smile. "He can just have the hat. It looks like he's getting more enjoyment out of that ugly old thing than I ever did! Would you just help me straighten up quickly?"

"Yeah, sure," Ace answered, standing the table back up while Nan picked the clothes up from the ground and started folding them.

"That sure is an interesting pet," said the woman, picking up the scattered shoes. "But, maybe you should put a leash on him or leave him at home when you're out."

"You're right," Ace agreed. "We just felt sorry for him being locked up in his pen all the time, now that he's too big to be in the house."

"Well, you're lucky he chose my sale to tear through," she said. "Someone else may not have been as understanding."

The woman was suddenly very chatty. "You know, it's too bad your pig got so big. Maybe you should think about sending him to live on a farm where he will have more room to run."

"Oh, Jack would never part with Chubbs," Nan said.

The woman smiled at her, knowingly. "Well, you kids look thirsty after chasing that pig. Would you like something to drink?" She opened a refrigerator in the garage, brought out a handful of juice boxes and passed them around.

"Thank you," they chorused.

"Is your friend going to come back and join the party?" she asked.

Jack waved to Millie, who slowly wandered back. Nan began to straighten the stacks of clothing on the table while Kara and Ace picked up several garden decorations and arranged them neatly into rows.

"Oh, pretty!" Kara exclaimed over a small gray rock with leaves carved into it and a word etched into its top. "What does it say?"

The woman read it to her.

– Decide! –

"A friend of mine gave this me to me a long time ago," she said. "I was having a hard time making a decision and…see here…

the seeds symbolize making a choice. She wanted me to remember that once a seed decides to grow, the rest comes naturally."

"I never thought of a seed deciding to grow," said Nan.

"Well, it's just a metaphor," the woman explained. "Before you make a decision to do something, the idea is kind of like a seed. It just lies there, doing nothing, until you decide to do something with it. Once you make the decision, the idea grows into something more."

"That's pretty cool," said Nan.

"I think so, too. Deciding to take action is sometimes the hardest part. But, once you make a decision to do something, everything else seems to fall into place."

"Nan, I want to buy it," Kara pleaded.

"Do you want that rock for your collection?" Ace asked her.

"Yes, but I don't have any money," Kara said with an exaggerated frown, kicking the ground with her shoe.

Ace fished into his pocket and pulled out two quarters. "Will you take fifty cents for that rock?" he asked.

"Sure," she answered.

"Thank you, Ace!" Kara's eyes lit up as Ace handed the rock over to her.

"Well, we should probably get going," Ace told the woman. "Thanks for the juice."

"Yeah, and for being so nice about the mess," Nan added. "Are you sure you don't want us to pay for that hat?"

"Don't worry about it," the woman answered. "Just take that pig home before he gets you into any more trouble, okay?"

"We will," Jack agreed as they walked away.

"Let's go quick, before anything else happens," Ace hissed, leading the others back toward his house.

"Wait!" Millie protested. "We still have seven more sales to go to!"

"Millie, I hardly think that's a priority right now!" Nan scolded her. "Chubbs has reached his limit and it's time to get him home."

Millie stopped and began to yell at them. "Oh, great! You just had to bring that stupid pig along, and now look! I knew this was going to happen!"

She struggled not to cry.

Ace reasoned with her. "What if Nan and I take Chubbs back home while you and Jack go on? That way, we can get Chubbs out of the way and the two of you can still hit the rest of the sales. It's past lunchtime anyway, and I'm getting hungry."

"Me, too!" Kara piped up.

"Well..." Millie hesitated.

"Are you sure you can handle Chubbs?" Jack asked.

"Sure," Ace replied. "Go on, we'll see you at home later."

"Well, alright," Jack relented. "Let's go Millie. It will be faster with just the two of us anyway."

"Fine!" Millie said. "Let's just go."

She turned and stomped away with Jack at her heels while the other three led Chubbs quietly home.

⋆ ⋆ ⋆ ⋆ ⋆

Kara was excited to show off her newest rock when her mother got home late from work that evening.

Ms. Webster carefully turned the rock in her hands. "Well, that's obviously a very special rock, Kara. I like the carvings on it, too! What do you think you're going to do with all of these rocks?"

"I don't know," Kara answered. "I can put them in a box under my bed when I'm not looking at them."

Ms. Webster was thoughtful. "It seems a shame to keep them buried under your bed when they are all so full of wisdom.

It would be nice if we could share them with other people somehow."

"Yeah," Kara answered. "The lady that sold it to me told me what it means."

"Really?"

"Yeah, she said that seeds can grow into bigger things, like ideas."

Nan smiled. "That's not exactly what she said."

"That's interesting," said Ms. Webster. "Making decisions can be a big deal."

"Yup!" Kara answered.

"Hmmm."

"*Now* what are you thinking about, mom?" Nan asked.

"Well, I was just thinking about an idea that I've had for quite a while. Maybe it's time to stop thinking about it and just do it."

"Oh no," Nan moaned. Nan didn't want to hear another idea that would get her hopes up for something great. Not tonight.

CHAPTER 9

# Keeping It Together

They were all sprawled miserably across various pieces of furniture in the Emerson's living room.

Nan had decided to write a story about the summer and was writing in her journal. She began with "We were wallowing in the oppressive haze of defeat that seemed to permeate the air around us." She wasn't exactly sure what it meant but she liked the way it sounded!

"Argh…" Millie groaned quietly, burying her face in a big, striped, squishy pillow on the sofa.

"This stinks!" Ace exclaimed suddenly. "Millie, let's just go to your house and swim in the pool while you still have it!"

Jack glared at his stepbrother and Nan was appalled at his blatant insensitivity, even though the thought of using Millie's pool one last time did sound great.

"Ace! I can't believe you just said that!" said Nan.

Kara patted Millie's arm in reassurance. "Don't worry, Millie. We'll think of something. Right, guys?" Her sweet eyes questioned the others, begging for support.

Ace breathed a sigh of remorse. "I'm sorry, Millie," he told her. "Of course we'll think of something."

"Yeah," Jack added, not to be outdone. "Why don't we look online at some of those auction websites and classified ads? There has to be something there."

"I'll grab the newspaper," Ace said.

Nan sat and watched as Jack, Millie, and Kara went into the next room to sit at the computer. "Ugh," she thought to herself. If things were so serious, why weren't Millie's parents doing something about it? She had just seen Mrs. Medlin stroll out of the house with Mrs. Emerson that morning, apparently on their way to the spa. Mrs. Medlin wore designer clothes, as usual, and carried a brand new handbag.

Nan couldn't help wondering if Mrs. Medlin might deserve to lose her house if all she cared about was spending money on things she didn't need at all. Why shouldn't it be Mrs. Medlin forking over her spending money and wasting her summer running around looking for treasure to save her house. Nan was having a hard time feeling sorry for either Millie or her mother. In fact, she thought they might just learn something from losing their home.

"Here," said Ace, interrupting her thoughts. "I'll take the front of the classified section, and you take the back part."

"Don't you think this is all just a little bit pointless?" Nan whined. She flopped over against the pillow that Millie had just abandoned. Nan could hear Jack and Millie's voices droning on in the dining room.

"What do you mean?" Ace asked.

"Well, for one thing, what do we even know about antiques? How are we going to know if we've found something that's worth any money?"

"I don't know," Ace replied. "I guess we're just hoping something will pop out at us."

"But, if it pops out at us, don't you think it will pop out at someone else first?"

"I guess," Ace said. "Look, I just don't want to sit and watch Millie mope around like it's the end of the world. At least we're doing something."

Nan rolled her eyes and opened her section of the paper. "Yeah, we're doing something alright...wasting our time! We haven't done anything fun this summer at all, and for what? Even if we do end up finding something, Millie and her mother will probably just take the money and go on a huge shopping spree! Don't you ever think that maybe they deserve what's happening to them?"

"Really?" Ace asked. "You don't really think that."

"You don't know what I think," Nan argued.

"Well, you want to know what I think? I think maybe you're just a little bit jealous of Millie."

"Jealous?!" Nan laughed self-consciously. "You don't know what you're talking about!"

"Don't I?"

"No, you don't!" Nan argued, jumping up from her seat. She took her half of the newspaper, went into the next room and sat at the dining room table.

"What about baseball cards?" Jack was asking Millie as Nan entered the room.

"Maybe," she answered doubtfully.

"You find anything yet?" Nan asked.

"Not really," Millie answered.

"Well, actually," Jack added, "it's more like we've found too much. There's just so much stuff to go through, and I have no idea how you figure out what's worth looking at. It all looks like junk to me."

Nan began to look through the classified ads.

"Oh, what about that?" Millie asked, pointing to a picture of a collection of unopened baseball cards. "It's cheap and maybe we'll get lucky and find some really rare card in it."

Jack shrugged his shoulders and clicked the "Add to Cart" icon.

Ace came in and sat right next to Nan. She turned her back to him. She was not in a forgiving mood. Ace grabbed her part of the paper in a flirty sort of way. Even in her defensive stance she could feel it.

"I think I have to register for an account before I can buy anything," Jack told Millie.

Millie sat at the table next to Ace while Jack began to fill out the online registration form. "You find anything in the paper?" she asked him.

"Mostly used mattresses and old recliners," Ace replied. "More junk."

Millie sighed while Ace continued to look through the rest of the paper. Suddenly, Jack sighed loudly.

"What's wrong?" Kara asked.

"I gotta have a credit card to complete the registration."

"So, just borrow your mom's credit card," Millie shrugged nonchalantly. "That's what I always do."

"You use your mom's credit card?" Nan said, not believing anyone could be that stupid. She didn't even know if her mother had a credit card. And if she did, there was no way Nan would ever attempt to use it.

"So?" Millie said. "What's the big deal?"

"What's the big deal?!" Ace was incredulous. "Are you kidding me?"

"No..." Millie replied, furrowing her brow quizzically.

Even Jack was taken aback. "Aren't you afraid you'll get in trouble?"

"Who cares?" Millie said bluntly. "It's not as if my mom has any idea what's going on with the credit cards anyway. She just hides the bills from my dad without even opening them."

"Oh, my gosh," Nan almost whispered. "You're serious."

"What do you all think credit cards are for?" Millie continued.

"Well, there's no way I'm borrowing my mom's credit card without asking her," Jack replied, still looking at Millie strangely. "I would be grounded for life!"

"My dad doesn't believe in credit cards," said Ace. "He always says 'If you can't afford it in cash, you can't afford it at all' and 'Using credit cards is all about instant gratification, but there's nothing gratifying about credit card bills.'"

"Yeah," Jack answered. "But he also says 'Only borrow money when it's going to make you money.' And if we buy something we can sell for a lot more money, then we're only borrowing money to make money, right?"

Nan thought it was interesting that Jack was starting to quote his stepfather.

Ace scowled. "Somehow, I don't think that's what my dad meant, Jack. So just drop it…unless, of course, you'd like to borrow your mother's credit card after all?"

"No," Jack stated. "For once, I think you may be right, Ace. It's just not going to work. We'll have to think of something else."

"So, what are we going to do then?" Millie's voice was beginning to get that high-pitched tone that usually warned of an impending meltdown.

"Calm down," Ace warned her. "Why don't you bookmark that page, for now, and move on to the classified ads? If you find something nearby then maybe we can pay cash for it when we go pick it up."

"Good idea," Jack added quickly.

Ace leaned toward Nan and whispered into her ear. "I'm sorry," he told her. "I think I see what you mean."

"Thank you." Nan grabbed the newspaper from Ace and began to look through it again.

"Junk, junk, junk!" Millie's voice climbed as she exclaimed over the classified listings they were finding. "Doesn't anyone have anything to sell that's worth anything?"

"Oh, wait!" Nan interrupted, holding up a sheet of newspaper. "What about an auction? I bet there's some good stuff there!"

"Let me see that." Millie snatched the paper from Nan's outstretched hand. "Collectables," she read, "that sounds promising."

"Yeah," Ace added. "One time, on that antique show that my dad watches, there was this guy who found a necklace in the bottom of a box of junk at an auction. He bought the entire box for fifty cents, or a quarter, or something, and the necklace ended up being worth $50,000."

"When is it?" Jack asked.

"This afternoon!" Millie was beginning to get excited, but her face quickly fell as she read on. "Oh, but look where it is! It's way out in the country. There's no way we can get there on the bus!" she wailed, and threw herself dramatically into a chair.

Jack looked at Ace. "Do you think your dad would take us?"

"We can ask," Ace replied. "But I know he's pretty busy right now."

"Let's go ask him!" Millie jumped out of her chair again with renewed hope.

Although Nan was beginning to fear for Millie's sanity, she got up from her seat to follow her out the back door and onto the patio. Jack, Ace, and Kara were close behind her.

"Mr. Emerson!" Millie called out across the back yard.

Chubbs squealed from his pen, hoping for some attention. "Shut up, you stupid pig!" Millie screamed at him. "MR. EMERSON!!"

"Millie!" Jack and Ace yelled together.

"Jeez, Millie! Calm down!" Nan exclaimed, embarrassed.

Mr. Emerson came from the garage, wiping his big, greasy hands on a shop rag. "What's wrong?" he asked, concerned. "Is everyone all right?"

"Mr. Emerson!" Millie ran to him breathlessly, but stopped short when she noticed how dirty he was. "Mr. Emerson, we were just wondering if you could do a teeny, tiny little favor for us."

"I can try," Mr. Emerson answered doubtfully. "It just depends on how teeny tiny this little favor is." He looked at his son and winked.

"Mr. Emerson," Millie gushed. "We really, really want to go to this auction this afternoon but it's too far out of town for us to take the bus, and we were wondering if you would drive us...please, we would really appreciate it, and we won't be any trouble at all!"

"This afternoon, huh?"

"Yes, it's this afternoon," Millie continued, then eyed his filthy shirt with disgust. "And it starts in an hour so you might just have time to clean up really fast before we have to leave."

"Gosh, I'm really sorry, Millie," Mr. Emerson told her. "But, I'm having some problems with my truck and I really need to get it fixed this afternoon. And even if I didn't, I couldn't take all of you anywhere. There aren't enough seat belts."

Millie's face fell.

Mr. Emerson obviously felt bad for disappointing her. "But, hey," he continued, "I think the big flea market is going on next week. I'll make sure Mrs. Emerson leaves me the van that day and I'll take you all to the fair grounds. I think you'll like that better than an auction anyway."

"Thanks, Dad!" Ace grinned.

"And I have an even better idea," Mr. Emerson went on. "What would you all say to going to the beach tomorrow?"

Nan's spirits rose. Finally, something fun! "That would be great!" she said.

"Awesome!" Ace exclaimed.

"Yeah," Jack answered. "We could bring the metal detector along with us and see if we can find stuff in the sand while we're there!"

Millie brightened up, too.

"Be here at 9:00 tomorrow morning," Mr. Emerson told them as he headed back toward the garage. "Oh, wait." He stopped and reached into his pocket. "I almost forgot. I have something for you, Kara."

"For me?" Kara asked, astonished.

Mr. Emerson took Kara's hand and placed something in her palm. "Yes, for you," he said, smiling. "For your collection."

Nan appreciated Mr. Emerson more and more. She wondered if all policemen were so caring. She watched intently as Kara opened her hand and looked at the rock that Mr. Emerson had placed there. It was a smooth, glossy gray with black marbling. And there, on the flat surface, was yet another inscription.

"Oh, thank you, Mr. Emerson!" Kara exclaimed, grinning from ear to ear.

"No problem," Mr. Emerson grinned in return. "You kids stay out of trouble now, you hear?"

Nan rolled her eyes. There was that "trouble" thing again. She hoped he wasn't "imagining" anything!

"Yes, sir!" Ace replied.

"Let me see your rock, Kara," Jack said. "What does it say?"

Kara handed the rock over to Jack. "Here, read it," she said.

Jack squinted his eyes and turned to block the sun that was glaring on the rock's shiny surface.

– Be Persistent –

"What's persistent?" Kara asked.

"Um, being persistent…" Jack began.

"It means to keep going," Nan jumped in. "You know, like you just keep trying and trying and don't give up."

"Oh," said Kara, far more interested in the rock than the words.

"Right," said Jack. "Remember the planning? You don't quit, you make a new plan."

Ace added his two cents. "As long as you keep trying you will win no matter what."

"I don't think that's true," Nan argued, glancing toward Millie. "Just because we keep trying to find this stupid treasure doesn't mean it's ever going to happen. I mean, if there's no treasure to be found then it doesn't matter how persistent you are."

"Oh, you're a big help." Millie reprimanded.

"Yeah," Jack defended Millie. "With that attitude, we'll definitely never find anything."

Nan stared at her feet. If she didn't say something now, she might never. "It just doesn't seem like anything we've done has worked. It feels like we're missing something really important here, and I am tired of wasting my time."

"What do you mean, 'we're missing something?'" Jack prodded her.

Nan hesitated, not completely convinced she should share her fears about Millie and her mother taking the treasure and blowing it. "Well..." she started. "We're working so hard to find this 'treasure,' but then what? What's the plan after that? Do we just turn the money over to Millie and hope for the best?"

"What exactly are you trying to say, Nan?" Millie asked.

Nan dug her feet in. "I just wonder what *exactly* you're planning to do with the money, if we do ever find anything."

"I told you," Millie said. "I need the money to save my house."

"But, what about the pony and the tiaras?" Kara asked. Nan looked quickly to her little sister, surprised that she had picked up on her feelings.

"Yeah, what about the pony and tiaras?" Ace echoed.

"Wha...what does that have to do with anything?!" Millie sputtered.

Jack glanced around at his friends fearfully. "Um, guys…we were talking about persistence?"

"We'll get to that, Jack." Ace held up a hand, gesturing him to stop. "Millie, we just want to know that we're not wasting our time finding you a bunch of money just so you can run out and buy a pony."

Nan looked at Ace gratefully. She was glad she wasn't the only one who felt that way.

"Oh, get real!" Millie glowered. "I made that comment about the pony and the tiaras before you knew about my house. I just didn't want you to know what was really going on!"

Nan looked at Ace and back to Millie, doubtful.

"Oh, come on!" Millie went on in a rush. "I just want to save my house. You guys are being ridiculous!"

"But, Millie," Ace tried to reason with her gently. "How did your family get in this situation anyway? I mean, if you and your mom just spend money like crazy and hide it from your dad, what's going to keep it from happening again?"

"You don't know what you're talking about!" Millie turned on her heel and stalked away. Ace had obviously hit a nerve.

"Millie, wait!" Jack called after her. He turned angrily to Ace and Nan. "Now look what you did! Some friends you are!"

Ace and Nan watched as Jack ran after Millie.

"Do you think we should go after them?" Ace asked.

Nan threw her hands into the air. "Oh, I don't know!"

Kara seemed to come to a decision on her own and ran after Millie and Jack. Ace only paused long enough to raise an eyebrow at Nan before he followed, as well.

"Oh, wait for me!" Nan called out, breaking into a run.

"Millie, where are you going?" Kara called.

Half a block away, Millie slowed to a walk, then stumbled to the ground and buried her face in her hands. First Jack, and then Kara caught up to her and sat next to her, patting her back.

"We're sorry, Millie," said Kara, trying to console her.

"Millie," Ace gasped. He bent over, bracing himself with his hands against his knees.

"Why don't you two just go away?!" Millie screamed at Ace and Nan. "You don't care about me at all!"

"What is wrong with you?" Jack asked them. "Millie is our friend, and she needs our help. Why would you say those things to her?"

"I'm sorry," Ace mumbled, still acting as if he was catching his breath. "I want to help you, I really do."

Nan couldn't believe it. Ace was changing his story and leaving her all alone as the enemy.

"You have a great way of showing it!" Millie sobbed. "And you!" She turned to Nan. "You've never liked me! You never wanted to help from the beginning! You'll be happy to laugh at me when I'm homeless!"

"Oh my gosh!" Nan protested. "That's not true!" Suddenly, the whole thing had blown up in her face and she didn't know how. "I just don't know if this whole treasure hunt is really going to help anything," she added, trying to find her footing again.

"You know, maybe this is all *your* fault!" Millie accused Nan.

"My fault?" Nan was stunned. "How could any of this be my fault? You're crazy!"

"Oh, am I?" Millie asked, going on the offensive. "Maybe it's your lack of persistence that's keeping us from succeeding! Maybe, just maybe, you doomed us to fail from the very beginning. Did you ever think of that?"

"I…what?!" Nan didn't know how to respond.

"Just read the stupid rocks!" Millie told her. "You've been ready to quit every time things haven't gone perfectly. You're just negative, negative, negative. Nothing is possible around you, Nan!"

Nan looked to Ace for help but he kept his mouth clamped shut. She couldn't really blame him. Either way he would lose.

"Look," said Jack, grabbing each of the girls by the arm and pulling them toward each other. "We're all friends here. Millie, you know Nan wants to help you. And Nan, you know Millie wouldn't go to all of this trouble for a pony and a tiara. She needs help for real and we have to be here for her."

Nan tried not to look at Millie. She knew she should apologize, but she still thought she was right. She really did feel bad for Millie but she couldn't shake her feelings that Millie was selfish and spoiled. The silence was going on too long, though, and she gave in. "I'm sorry, Millie," Nan mumbled, looking at the grass under Jack's feet. She didn't know what else to say.

"Sorry for what, exactly?" Millie asked.

"I'm just…" Nan started. She did not like being on the spot like this and felt more uncomfortable than any amount of summer heat. Nan thought for another moment. She didn't want to pretend anymore. "Well, I guess I'm sorry for not being as helpful as I could have been."

Millie sniffled. "What difference does that make?"

Nan tried to explain. "Well, you can believe that I want to help you even if I don't happen to think that finding treasure is going to take care of everything."

Millie relented a bit. "Well, then, what *do* you think would help?"

Nan sighed. And then it hit her! "I think it would help to go talk to my mom." She didn't know why but for some reason she just knew her mother would know how to make everyone feel better.

"Yeah, let's do that," Jack decided. "There's nothing else we can do today, anyway. Tomorrow we can make a fresh start when we go to the beach."

Ace backed him up. "That sounds like a good idea," he said. "We'll all get back to work tomorrow."

"All of us?" Millie asked, looking at Nan.

"Yes, all of us," Nan replied, grateful for the chance to redeem herself. "What do I know anyway?"

CHAPTER 10

# Hidden Treasures

"Mom?" Nan called out into the dim apartment where she had expected to find her mother. "Mom, are you here?"

Kara ran in and jumped into the beanbag chair and turned on the television.

Nan's friends followed her into the kitchen and looked around curiously.

"Phew!" Millie fanned herself in the heat of the tiny, oppressive apartment. "Don't you people believe in air conditioning?"

Nan's face got hot and she felt like she would explode. After everything that just happened, she couldn't believe Millie could be so insensitive. But then, it would never occur to Millie that she might be the one hurting someone's feelings. Nan wished she hadn't thought of this at all.

Jack seemed to sense this and stepped in. "Let's find your mom," he said with encouragement.

Nan walked to the small, magnetic whiteboard that hung on the refrigerator. "She's down in the laundry room," Nan said, reading the note. "We might as well go down there."

"Down where?" Millie paused for a moment. "You mean, down in the basement?"

"Well yeah, that's where the laundry room is," Nan replied.

"Ugh, I hate basements," Millie informed her. "And I can only imagine what the basement of this place looks like."

Nan's temper flared.

"Basements are usually pretty cool," said Ace, stepping in to save Nan.

"Yeah, it'll definitely be cooler," added Jack.

Nan took a deep breath. "Fine," she said. "Let's go. Come on, Kara."

Nan held the door open as everyone filed out. Ace fell back, glancing around the apartment without realizing that Nan was staring at him until she cleared her throat loudly.

"See anything you like?" Nan asked sarcastically. She closed the door after Ace as he slipped out into the shabby hallway.

"I was just curious to see where you live," Ace answered sincerely. "I mean, I've been to Millie's tomb of a house plenty of times, but this is the first time you've ever invited me to your place."

"What's the big deal?" Nan asked, embarrassed and defensive. "It's just a crappy old apartment building. What was it you called it…an eyesore?"

Before Ace could reply, a little blonde boy, about Kara's age, tore through the hallway almost knocking him over. "Hey, watch it!" Ace called.

"Nannie's got a boyfriend!" the little boy sang, then stuck out his tongue at the two of them before disappearing into the elevator.

Nan and Ace looked at each other, then quickly away, both of their faces flushed.

"Who was that?" Ace asked.

"Just one of the brats from 210," Nan answered, walking quickly down the hall ahead of Ace. "I hope he gets stuck in the elevator."

Ace hurried to catch up to Nan who was already heading down the stairwell and into the dim light of the basement. There was a loud crash in the recesses of the basement, followed by muffled cursing just as Ace's feet hit the gray concrete floor of the lower level.

Nan and Ace entered the laundry room where their friends stood watching the commotion.

"Stupid machine!" A slovenly man of an undeterminable age was dragging his dripping wet laundry out of an ancient-looking washing machine and dumping it into a basket. He slammed the door of the machine and snatched his basket. "I'm going to the Laundromat!" he exclaimed to no one in particular. Water poured through the openings in the man's laundry basket and left a little stream trailing behind him as he left the room.

Nan's friends looked at each other apprehensively, but the adults in the room just laughed and went about their business. An elderly woman with short gray hair and wire-rimmed glasses grabbed a mop and began to clean up the mess. She looked up at Nan. "And, who is this young man?" she asked, with a funny little smile on her face.

"Hi, Mrs. Thompson," Nan replied, dutifully. "This is my friend Ace. He's Jack's stepbrother."

"Just Jack's stepbrother, eh?" said Mrs. Thompson with a wink at Ace that made Nan blush.

Nan gave Ace a nudge forward, ushering him farther into the room. "Ace, that's Mrs. Fitzgerald with my mom, and that's Mrs. Davis," she said, pointing to the folding table in the corner. "The brat's mother," she added with a whisper.

"Hello kids," Ms. Webster said as she put a load of her own laundry into the recently abandoned washing machine. "That man just doesn't know how to treat her," she explained, slamming the lid shut, pushing a button, and giving the machine a swift, strategic kick that started it right up. "He'll be one of the first to go."

"Uh-huh," Mrs. Thompson agreed.

Mrs. Fitzgerald, Mrs. Thompson's best friend in the building, also nodded her head. Mrs. Davis only lowered her face over her laundry.

"Mom, why are you all down here?" asked Nan.

"Oh, just thought we'd have a laundry fest," joked Ms. Webster. "What are you all up to?"

Just then, the holy terror from upstairs ran into the laundry room, nearly knocking Ace over for a second time.

"David Davis!" Mrs. Thompson reprimanded. "You'd better slow it down young man!"

David stopped in his tracks and stared up at the formidable woman who was still wielding the mop.

"Yes, ma'am," he answered contritely, looking to his mother.

"David, what are you doing down here by yourself?" Mrs. Davis asked him. She looked more haggard than embarrassed. "Where are your brothers?"

"I dunno," he shrugged, avoiding her gaze.

"What do you mean you don't know?" Mrs. Davis asked sternly. Her words sounded worried but her face just looked tired. "Why are you running around the building by yourself?"

"Danny locked me out."

"Locked you out?" Mrs. Thompson jumped in. "What are those brothers of yours up to now?" She looked toward Mrs. Davis who was quickly tossing her half-folded laundry into a basket and gathering her laundry supplies. She tucked the basket under one arm, and grabbed her young son by the wrist.

"Ow!" David cried. "I didn't do anything! It was Dustin's idea! I just said I wanted a slip and slide. He's the one that dumped the soap all over the floor!"

"What?" exclaimed his mother.

Mrs. Davis looked absolutely dumbfounded at that piece of information, which Nan didn't understand at all. Those boys were always into trouble. Why their mother seemed surprised was beyond her.

Mrs. Davis dragged her son out of the laundry room, kicking and screaming. They could hear his cries all the way up the stairs.

Ace looked at Nan.

"I know!" replied Nan, sure of what he was thinking.

"Why does that woman continue to leave those kids alone when they act that way?" Nan's mom wondered aloud. "It's obvious the oldest boy can't control them. She looked at her daughters and smiled proudly. "I'm glad you girls know better than to act that way."

"Oh, please, Mom!" said Nan.

"Now, don't be too hard on Darla," Mrs. Thompson admonished. "Those boys aren't easy! And, as hard as one has to work to make ends meet, she's even worse off. It's not fair to expect so much from Darwin. He's only 16. He should be out running around and being a kid himself instead of being stuck playing father to his brothers. It's just a hard situation all around."

"I suppose," Ms. Webster acknowledged.

Suddenly one of the dryers began to make an awful clatter. "What the...?" Mrs. Fitzgerald jumped up and opened the machine where her clothes were supposed to be drying. She pulled out a wet towel and held it up with a sigh. "We may as well just put up a clothes line out back. I don't suppose Mr. Gizewski will be interested in giving me my money back on this load?"

"Ha!" Ms. Webster snorted. "Someday..."

"Mom!" Nan interrupted. She knew where her mother was going with this line of thought and was embarrassed to have her friends get another chance to see what an impractical dreamer she was.

"I'm just saying..."

"MOM!"

Nan's friends looked back and forth between her and her mother. Nan swallowed hard.

Ms. Webster continued despite her daughter's protests. "When I own this building, I won't make my tenants live this way. I mean, just think of the savings to the building in general if these ancient appliances were replaced with newer, energy efficient models. Anyone with any amount of business sense would take one look at this laundry room and run the other way."

"Mom, please..." Nan gently pleaded, trying to think of a way to change the subject.

Thankfully for Nan, Mrs. Fitzgerald came to her rescue. "So, what are you kids up to today, besides hanging out with a gaggle of old geese in the laundry room?" she asked.

"Speak for yourself," said Ms. Webster, good-naturedly.

"We're searching for treasure!" Kara eagerly informed her. Nan would have been happier if they just left.

"Really?" Mrs. Fitzgerald asked. "What kind of treasure are you looking for?"

"Ant keys," Kara told her.

"Ant keys?"

"She means antiques," Millie corrected.

"And, we're not really looking for treasure," Nan added. She didn't want to be an open book, like her mom. "We just saw one of those antique shows where people find out that their old junk is worth lots of money, and we were just curious to see what we could find."

"I see," said Mrs. Fitzgerald.

"Is that what you've been doing at the rummage sales?" Ms. Webster asked. "And here, I thought you were trying to save me some money by buying your own clothes."

"Mo-om!" Nan couldn't take any more embarrassment.

"Well, I'll tell you what," said Mrs. Fitzgerald, abandoning her soaking wet laundry and herding the children out of the laundry room. "You kids come with me. I think I might know where you can find some antiques. I can't guarantee that you'll be able to pry them away from Mr. G. if you find something good, but let's go see anyway."

"I wonder what she's up to," Nan's mother said to Mrs. Thompson.

Nan didn't care what she was up to as long as the attention moved off of her!

* * * * *

The dim, dusty storage room was full of ghostly white shapes of various sizes. Mrs. Fitzgerald and the children cautiously lifted the white sheets one at a time to peer at the furniture underneath.

Ms. Webster walked to one particularly large object and pulled the covering off with one swift jerk. She coughed at the dust that was stirred up in the air, then gasped at what she saw underneath. "Would you look at that marble? Where did this come from?"

"That was the original lobby desk," Mrs. Thompson answered. "I know you'd never guess it to look at the place now, but this building was pretty fancy at one time. When Mr. G. took over, he thought it was all outdated and too much work to restore. I think he emptied the lobby so people wouldn't hang out there!"

"I can't believe he never tried to sell any of this," Mrs. Fitzgerald said.

Mrs. Thompson answered her, shaking her head. "You know how lazy he is. I'm sure he just forgot all about it."

"This really wouldn't be all that difficult to restore," Ms. Webster thought aloud. "Can you just imagine the lobby with all of this beautiful, old furniture, completely refurbished…and a door man in a slick uniform behind the desk to keep watch over the place?"

"Can you just imagine the storage room we could free up down here if we cleaned this basement out?" Mrs. Fitzgerald added. "I mean, that would be an extra selling point, wouldn't it? I can just picture a couple of rows of storage cages filling this space, one for each unit…and then maybe an area for the kids to park their bikes so they don't have to leave them outside or drag them into their apartments."

"That is a great idea," Ms. Webster nodded her head thoughtfully. She moved away from the lobby desk to see what the kids were looking at.

Kara was wiping a layer of dust from the glass front of a large cabinet in an attempt to see inside. "I wonder what was in here," she said.

"It looks like some type of display case," Ms. Webster answered, looking the cabinet over thoughtfully.

"Ouch!"

Everyone turned to see Ace hopping on one foot, holding the other in his hand and grimacing in pain.

"Oh, now what did you do?" Jack asked, annoyed.

"Seriously, Ace," Millie added. "You are such a klutz for someone who is supposed to be such a great athlete!"

"I was just trying to pull a sheet off this chair, and I didn't see the rock on it 'til it landed on my foot!" Ace bent over to pick something up and stood proudly holding a large, gray stone for everyone to see. "Hey, hey, hey!" he exclaimed. "Would you look at this? It's got writing on it, Kara!"

Kara ran to him excitedly. "Lemme see, lemme see!"

"Hold on a minute." Ace held the rock up to the light and read what was written on it.

– Use Many Minds –

"What the heck does *that* mean?" Nan wondered out loud.

"Yeah, what the heck?" Jack asked.

The three adults glanced at each other thoughtfully.

Mrs. Fitzgerald was the first to speak. "Have you ever noticed that when you get together to talk about something with someone else, you learn more about the subject than you knew before?"

"Sure. Of course," said Jack.

"Sure. Of course," mimicked Ace.

Jack gave him a shove. So did Nan!

Ace just laughed.

Mrs. Fitzgerald continued. "Using many minds is better than one!"

Mrs. Thompson joined in. "There's a name for that. My husband, may he rest in peace, was part of a Master Mind group for his business. It was a great way to come with ideas they could never have come up with on their own."

"Yes, when you put two or more minds together, they become something entirely new," Ms. Webster added.

"Makes sense to me," Mrs. Fitzgerald shrugged.

"Yes, and just imagine what you might come up with if you have a group of people all working toward the same thing," said Mrs. Thompson. She looked meaningfully between Mrs. Fitzgerald and Ms. Webster.

"I guess you could consider us a Master Mind group," said Ms. Webster, grinning.

Mrs. Fitzgerald laughed. "I like the sound of that!" she said.

All the children looked at the adults as though they had lost their minds.

Nan sighed. She supposed they always stood around talking this way.

"We do make a great team," Mrs. Thompson said. "We all have the same goal but we're coming at the problem from different directions so we can see every point of view."

"Well, I think the best Master Mind groups would require people of varying talents who can bridge the knowledge gaps," Ms. Webster said. "If it weren't for you two ladies, I might never have discovered this treasure down here."

Millie looked around quickly, probably trying to discover what treasure they were talking about. Nan didn't see much herself. The room was full of old, junky lobby furniture that should have been hauled off to the dump years ago.

"Oh, no!" Mrs. Fitzgerald exclaimed suddenly. "It looks like the Davis boys have found their way down here too."

Ms. Webster went to join her and stopped short in front of a pile of carved wood pieces. They actually looked pretty except for the chalk and pencil markings all over them. Nan could read a few of them easily. "David was here" and "Dustin stinks."

"Oh, those little delinquents!" Ms. Webster muttered angrily. "I'm going to make them come down here and scrub every piece of wood and refinish it! Maybe if they have to start cleaning up around here they'll take some pride in where they live and stop destroying everything they can get their grubby little hands on!"

"Oh, but that's up to their mother," Mrs. Fitzgerald told her. "And you know she's not likely to say anything to them."

Ms. Webster stood tapping her foot angrily on the floor, furrowing her brow in concentration. "Well, I am not about to put up with it! She'd *better* say something to them if she wants to keep living here!"

"Now, calm down," Mrs. Thompson hushed her. "Don't say anything you might regret later. I'm sure we can think of something together. Maybe there is some way to get those boys more involved with things around here so they feel like they have some kind of purpose."

"Well, I think what they really need is their mother," Mrs. Fitzgerald said. "I just wish there were some way she could make ends meet without working three different jobs. It would make a world of difference to those boys if they could have their mother around more. It must be really hard on them."

"I guess so," Ms. Webster relented. "Well, let's get out of here. I don't want to think about this mess right now. We'll come up with something."

"Wow," said Jack, looking at his watch. "It's a lot later than I thought! We'd better get home before we get in trouble."

"Yeah, we should probably go," Ace agreed.

Nan was pretty sure they just wanted an excuse to get out of there, but then, so did she!

CHAPTER 11

# Diamond in the Rough

Nan was surprised to see Chubbs squashed into the space between the two middle seats of the Emerson's van the next morning when she climbed in at 9:00 am on the dot. Jack and Millie sat in the back seat and Ace sat in front next to his father. Kara squealed with excitement. Chubbs replied with a piercing squeal of his own, and backed into Millie.

"Ow!" Millie cried, grabbing her foot. "Your stupid pig stepped on me, Jack! You just *had* to bring him along, didn't you?"

Jack gently tried to push Chubbs away from Millie, but there wasn't much room for him to move. "Aw, he didn't do it on purpose, Millie."

"How did you even manage to get him in here?" Nan asked.

"It wasn't easy!" Ace laughed.

"Is everyone buckled in?" Mr. Emerson asked as he pulled the van out into the street.

"Yes!" they chorused.

"Alright, then! We're off!"

It was less than an hour's drive to the beach and everyone was in high spirits, for a change! Kara chattered away to no one in particular, and Nan listened to Ace and his father discussing a fishing trip they were planning for the end of summer. Jack tinkered with his stepfather's metal detector in the back seat while Millie stared out the window. Before long, they were pulling into the parking lot, and the long, sandy beach was in sight.

"Yippee! Yippee! Yippee!" Kara exclaimed, bouncing up and down in her seat. Sometimes Nan found Kara to be so annoying.

Ace was opening his door before Mr. Emerson could shift the van into 'park'.

Nan jumped out of her own door and away from the van just in time to avoid being trampled by Chubbs, who practically leapt from the vehicle with Kara, Jack, and Millie close behind.

Mr. Emerson opened the back of the van and began to unload a bunch of beach gear. "Everyone grab an arm load and head down to the water," he told them, grabbing a large cooler while the kids gathered up the towels, beach toys, and other various necessities.

Ace dropped his arm load in the sand and ripped his shirt off as he ran into the water with a whoop and a splash. "Oh, yeah!" he yelled, bursting up and shaking water from his hair like a dog.

Nan helped her sister strip down to her bathing suit before spreading a towel in the sand and throwing her own clothes down. Jack and Millie immediately began to mess with the metal detector. Nan gave them one quick glance and then ran into the water after Kara and Ace before she could be sucked into more treasure hunting.

Mr. Emerson joined Nan, Kara, and Ace in the water for a while, splashing them and dunking Ace underwater. He called to his stepson and Millie a few times, trying to get them to join the fun but Jack pretended not to hear him, and Millie followed suit. The pair made their way down the beach with the metal detector, sweeping it back and forth in wide arcs.

Occasionally, Nan heard them cheer and watched them dig furiously in the sand but they didn't look like they were coming up with much at all.

Mr. Emerson left the water to sit in a lounge chair and relax. Kara soon followed and started to build a sand castle in the damp sand. That left Nan and Ace bobbing in the lake. Nan stole a glance at Ace and thought about her first impressions of him. It was funny how things could change. She had been so sure he was a jerk but now the same behavior she judged before just seemed normal. She actually *liked* hanging out with him.

Ace looked in Nan's direction and smiled which initiated a full-blown blush across her cheeks. When she felt the warmth in her face, she suddenly felt self-conscious and awkward.

"Let's see what Kara is up to," she stammered.

"Okay," he answered, and the two joined Kara on the beach.

"Wanna help build a sand castle?" Kara asked.

"Nah," Ace replied, picking up a shovel. "I'm gonna dig a big hole."

"Why?" Nan asked him.

"I don't know," he said. "I've always wanted to dig a big hole at the beach."

Nan grimaced and started digging a moat around Kara's castle. Boys were just different!

Ace started digging a few feet away, quickly throwing the excess sand in a pile next to him. He was standing about two feet into the ground when Jack and Millie finally returned to grab a soda from the cooler.

"What are *you* doing?" Millie asked, popping open her soda and giving Ace an annoyed look as she took a sip.

"Digging," Ace grunted, as he lifted another heaping shovel full of sand.

"Why?"

"Why not?"

"Well," Millie scolded, "if you really want to dig, you could at least come with us and dig up treasure instead of digging a huge stupid hole for no reason."

Ace paused long enough to glare at Millie until she shifted uncomfortably under his gaze, and then went back to his digging without saying another word.

"I'll come dig with you, Millie!" Kara jumped up and brushed the damp sand from her bathing suit.

"Whatever," said Millie, as she stalked away.

Mr. Emerson woke from his nap and looked up the beach. "I think that's Karl Fletcher," he said to Ace. "I'm gonna run over and say hello."

"Sounds good, Dad," said Ace, without stopping.

Nan claimed Mr. Emerson's seat after he jogged away and she sat back with her eyes closed to relax in the sun.

* * * * *

Nan wasn't sure how long she'd been asleep when her sister suddenly woke her with her excited yelling. "Nan! Nan! Wake up! Look what I found!"

"Come back here, you little brat!" Millie ran toward them with an angry scowl on her face, howling all the way.

Nan jumped up, feeling instantly protective of her sister. No one had the right to call Kara a brat, especially not Millie Medlin.

Jack was running after them, still awkwardly holding on to the metal detector.

"It's mine!" yelled Millie. "It's my treasure, and you can't have it!"

"It's not a treasure!" Kara yelled back at her, clutching something tightly to her chest. "It's a rock with writing on it, and I saw it first so I get to keep it!"

"Give it here!" Millie grabbed Kara's arms, trying to force the rock from her grip.

"Millie, stop it!" Ace exclaimed, climbing out of the hole that was now almost as deep as he was tall. He grabbed Millie from behind and then Jack grabbed Kara in an attempt to pull the two girls apart. Ace managed to release Millie's grip on Kara's arms, causing Jack to stumble backward over the mound of sand that Ace had piled up, sending both Kara and Jack backward into the hole.

"Kara!" Nan cried, running to her sister's aid. She reached into the deep pit and grabbed Kara's hand to pull her out, but suddenly, the sand shifted under her feet, and with no further warning, caved into the hole like a mini avalanche.

"Kara!" Nan screamed in horror, feeling her sister's small hand slipping from her grip as the sand began to fall in all around her, actually pulling her down.

"Nan?" Kara's eyes widened in fear, and Nan began to panic at the idea of her sister being buried alive. Jack started to panic too, trying to claw himself out of the hole but the sides caved in more and more with every handful.

Without hesitation, Ace laid his long body out and away from the sand hole so that he could reach in for Kara's hand while most of him was on more solid ground. He gripped her wrist hard. She screamed as he pulled…it was hard, but he managed to pull her up the side of the hole. Then, with all his strength, he pulled Kara as he moved his body back, grunting loudly until she was free.

Nan grabbed her and held her close. It felt like her heart had broken wide open and all her feelings were pouring out of her. She didn't even sense the tears that were running down her cheeks. She buried her face in Kara's shoulder. "I love you so much, Kara-bear," she whispered, "I thought you were gonna be buried alive!"

Kara melted into her big sister's arms and just trembled.

"Nan, help me!" Ace called frantically. "Go get my dad! Hurry!"

Nan lurched back into reality. "Oh my gosh, Jack!" she cried. She looked up to see that Ace had repositioned himself to pull Jack out of the sand as he had Kara, but it wasn't working.

Nan looked Kara squarely in the face. "Kara, everything's okay. I'll be right back. DON'T MOVE!"

Millie immediately went to Kara's side as Nan ran down the beach to find Mr. Emerson.

"Mr. Emerson! Mr. Emerson!" Nan screamed when she saw him ahead.

"Nan, what is it?" he called.

"Hurry, Jack's buried in the sand!"

Mr. Emerson took no time to think as he could tell by the look on Nan's face that something was terribly wrong. He broke out into a run toward his sons, with his friend following close behind. As soon as they were close enough to see what was happening, Mr. Emerson realized Jack was in a very deep hole.

"Jack!" he called, feeling the fear that was swirling around.

Mr. Emerson's friend made a quick assessment of the situation. "Stop digging!" he ordered. When he realized the kids were really scared, he spoke with a little less volume. "Look, it's important that we all stay calm. I know you're feeling afraid but the more you struggle, Jack, the more packed the sand will become around you. Don't worry, we'll get you out."

Nan heard Mr. Emerson's friend whisper under his breath. "This is serious, Jim. We have to do this carefully and quickly."

She shook and felt scared.

Mr. Emerson fell onto the ground next to the hole. "Jack, how are you doing?"

"I…can't…breathe." Jack gasped.

The heavy, damp sand must have been pressing against his chest.

"Help..." he said with tears streaming down his face.

Nan's heart broke open for the second time that afternoon, this time for her friend. Jack was probably the closest thing to a brother Nan would ever know. And here he was buried up to his armpits.

Mr. Emerson directed Jack to slowly move some of the sand from his chest area. "Make a moat around your body with just one finger...that's it. Stay close to your skin."

As Mr. Emerson continued to work with Jack, his friend organized a group of people who were suddenly gathered around. Some brought shovels, others had buckets in their hands. They all seemed ready to do whatever Mr. Fletcher asked.

Nan was amazed at how quickly it was all happening. She pulled Kara close.

Mr. Fletcher guided the people with shovels to clear as much sand as they could away from the hole. He said they needed to widen the hole layer by layer, to keep the sand from falling in.

As everyone worked, Mr. Emerson talked to Jack. Nan could hear his words of assurance in bits and pieces as he comforted Jack and kept him distracted.

Even though Mr. Emerson would have been a big help in moving the sand, he just kept talking to Jack. His entire focus was on making sure Jack was all right and staying calm.

Jack nodded his head a lot, which Nan took as a good sign. She followed Jack's every move and facial expression, as if staying connected to him would somehow keep him safe.

"Take a breath, Jack," Mr. Emerson said, "now let it out slowly...good."

Nan realized that she had been holding hers and also let out a deep sigh. Kara and Millie, who had been by her side for an hour, scooted in just a little closer. Nan took Millie's hand as the three watched...and hoped.

Nan thought about hope. It was more than a wish. It had substance to it. It felt more real. She thought about Mr. Emerson. He was helping Jack feel hope, she thought. He was helping Jack believe that he was going to be just fine. And maybe he was helping Jack believe that he was going to be okay in a bigger sense, too.

Nan heard Mr. Emerson say, "Not much longer," but to her it was taking forever.

The people kept digging the sand from around the hole. And all Jack could do was wait.

Just when it seemed like it was never going to end, Nan could see the top of Jack's bathing suit! She hadn't realized how much progress had actually been made. Her stomach fluttered.

And then things started to shift. Everyone threw their shovels off to the side and started lining up. At Mr. Fletcher's direction, they began to form a human chain. There was excitement in the air!

"We're going to have to pull fast when we do, so we need to be together on this," said Mr. Emerson's friend.

"Jack, when I give the word, we're gonna pull hard…your job is to hold the grip…that's all you have do. Understand?"

Jack nodded his head.

The people closest to the hole were low to the ground. The ones farther away were standing, anchored by the ones in the back. Mr. Emerson reached into the hold and took one of Jack's hands in a cross-grip to the forearm. His other hand was locked in to Mr. Fletcher in the same way. Ace was standing in the middle, ready with the others to move at Mr. Fletcher's signal.

"Hold on, Jack!" Mr. Emerson assured him. "We're gonna get you out of here, buddy. Just hold on tight."

Mr. Emerson's friend spoke loudly. "Okay, everyone. On the count of three, everyone's going to shift their weight backwards. Pick up the slack. Slowly, everyone. Okay, that's great. Just a little more…good!

"Okay, Jim, when you feel my grip tighten, pick up the slack on Jack and then pull. One…two…three!"

In one big explosive jolt, Mr. Emerson pulled Jack up and out of the hole. Jack landed in a face-plant but Mr. Emerson gathered him up into a big bear hug. Jack came up spitting out sand from his mouth. Tears ran down Mr. Emerson's face as he held Jack tightly.

The people who had gathered to make the rescue were cheering and slapping hands and hugging. It was like nothing Nan had ever seen before.

Millie brought Jack some water and everyone turned his attention to hear Jack's first words.

"I think I'm all right, but you're holding me too tight!"

"Oh, sorry," said Mr. Emerson and released his grip on Jack. Everyone cheered again.

Mr. Emerson kneeled over Jack, his face lined with worry. "Can you breathe now?"

"Yeah." Jack took a deep breath as if to prove to everyone, and himself, that he could in fact breathe. "Yeah. I'm good."

Just as soon as he took the next breath, though, Jack broke down and began to sob uncontrollably.

"It's okay, son," Mr. Emerson reassured Jack, putting an arm around him. "You're going to be just fine, now. Thank goodness you're okay."

Jack's sobs eventually subsided and people who had been complete strangers hours before shook his hand or gave him a hug before they went back to whatever they had been doing. Nan guessed that they would never quite be the same. She knew she wouldn't.

"Dude, that was a near-death experience," Ace blurted. Even though his comment didn't seem all that appropriate to Nan, she could tell that Ace's concern for his stepbrother was authentic. "You really scared me," Ace added.

Mr. Emerson opened an arm toward his son, inviting him into his arms for a group hug. Jack sighed and, at least for the moment, seemed to relax into his new family.

Nan felt really happy for Jack and Ace and Mr. Emerson and, for a split second, felt as though everything was perfect.

* * * * *

As Jack began to feel better, he became more himself and ready to move on.

"I'm fine, really," Jack assured everyone.

Nan, who was still holding Kara close at her side, noticed that her sister was clutching something in her little fist. "What did you guys find, anyway?" she asked.

Kara and Millie suddenly remembered what had started the commotion, and Kara held her newest treasure close against her chest. "A new rock for my collection!" Kara stated.

"We found the treasure!" Millie cried at the same time.

"No, it's a rock for my collection!" Kara argued.

"Whoa, whoa, hold it!" Mr. Emerson broke in. "Show me what you found, Kara."

Kara reluctantly gave up her newest find, and everyone gasped at the sight of the huge, clear, sparkly stone that Ace's father held up to the light.

"Wow," he said.

"Is that a diamond?" Ace asked in disbelief.

"It's mine!" Millie cried.

"But I found it!" Kara protested. "Please, Mr. Emerson! Tell her she has to let me keep it!"

Mr. Emerson tucked the stone into his pocket and looked sternly at the arguing girls. "I'm sorry, girls, but I can't possibly let either one of you keep this rock."

"What?!" Millie exclaimed in disbelief.

"I don't know if this is a real diamond or not, but it does have a name inscribed on it, and I am sure that someone is missing it," Ace's father explained. "You can't just keep something like this without first attempting to find out who it belongs to."

"He's right, girls," Mr. Emerson's friend backed him up. "If someone lost a rock like that, they probably filed a police report. It wouldn't be right to keep it."

"But Mr. Emerson…" Millie pleaded.

"No buts. I'm going take this back to the station tomorrow and see if anyone has reported it missing. If no one claims it within a certain period of time, then maybe you can keep it."

"And then I can add it to my collection?" Kara asked.

"No, it's mine!" Millie growled at her.

"No amount of arguing is going to change the situation," Mr. Emerson interrupted.

"Look, there's no use worrying about that now when it's just as likely that we're going to find the real owner and then it won't matter who found it first."

"Maybe you'll get lucky and there will be a reward," Ace suggested. Millie brightened up a bit at that idea.

"Jim, why don't you let me run a search tomorrow," Mr. Emerson's friend offered, "and I'll leave it on your desk for you. It may not even be a real diamond anyway."

Nan looked at the men with true admiration. They had been an amazing team.

"Thanks, Karl," Mr. Emerson said, and held out his hand to his friend. "Karl, thank you," he said with more emphasis. "You were a 'friend in deed' today."

The two men shook hands and exchanged a shoulder squeeze. "I'm glad I was here." He turned to the kids. "The rule is no holes deeper than your knees. Okay?"

Everyone nodded in agreement.

Jack held out his hand to Mr. Emerson's friend as well. "Thank you, sir," he said.

* * * * *

A few days later, Mr. Emerson took the kids into work with him to meet a lady who had reported a missing family heirloom the prior summer.

Millie and Kara sat across from each other at the small conference table where Mr. Emerson had left them. They were both upset over the loss of "their" rock. Nan was afraid to say anything for fear of setting Millie off. She had been unbearably moody, even for Millie. The sound of Ace drumming his fingers was the only sound in the room.

Finally, Ace's father entered the room with a frail old woman on his arm.

"Mrs. Fields," Mr. Emerson began, "let me introduce you to my sons and their friends." Jack lifted an eyebrow upon hearing his stepfather refer to him as his son rather than his stepson.

"Oh, I am so pleased I get to meet you all," the lady said with a friendly smile. "I can't tell you how much it means to me to have this diamond back. Of course, it's not a real diamond, but it's the first gift my late husband ever gave to me, and it means so much. I felt sick over losing it. I just can't believe that it has finally been returned! I don't have a clue how it ended up in the sand."

Millie appeared happy to find out it wasn't a real diamond she was losing. Kara, on the other hand, still looked disappointed.

"I thought you said it was a priceless heirloom," Jack said to his stepfather suspiciously.

"It's priceless alright," Mrs. Fields answered. "Oh, I know it might be worthless to most people, but it was in my husband's family for a long time before he gave it to me. And now, my one and only great-granddaughter is getting married, and I am so happy to have it back just in time to give it to her as a wedding gift."

She looked at Jack. "It's not priceless for the money that I could get out of it, but because of the loving memories it helps me keep alive."

"Oh," Jack said.

"Don't worry, Jack," Mr. Emerson said. "You'll understand someday."

Nan thought that Jack probably did understand. She knew he regretted throwing away his dad's mangled old horn.

"And, this lovely little girl must be Kara," Mrs. Fields said, placing a feather light hand on Kara's shoulder.

Kara looked up at her in surprise.

"Officer Emerson told me all about your rock collection."

"He did?"

"Oh, yes. And, I hear this rock of mine would have made an excellent addition."

Kara looked up, hopefully, at the elderly woman.

Everyone watched Mrs. Fields expectantly as she reached into her handbag. "I wonder if this will do in exchange," she said, handing something to Kara.

"What is it?" Jack asked, craning his head to see.

"A rock." Kara held it up for all to see, a grin working its way across her face. She looked at it and squealed. "Look! It has writing on it!"

Kara handed the rock to Nan, patiently waiting for her to read the inscription on the smooth surface of the large, chocolate brown stone.

– Let Love Be Your Guide –

"I thought you should have a special rock to replace the one that you returned to me," Mrs. Fields explained.

"Wow, thank you!" Nan said for her sister, who was too much in awe of this unexpected surprise to say anything. "Can you tell us about it?"

"Oh, yes," said Mrs. Fields. "My husband made this for me many years ago and I'd like to pass its message on to you. The message is this: whatever you do, wherever you go, you must let love be your guide.

"Love steps up the vibrations of the mind," she said, "and starts the wheels of physical action. If you use the power of love wisely, you can accomplish anything. Without it, though, your desires may get out of control and lead you astray.

"Remember to let love soften your passions so that you stay true to yourselves and love others along the way."

Mrs. Fields paused to look at each one of them individually. "Love changes everything," she added.

Nan gazed at Mrs. Fields with admiration. She imagined her as a queen who was giving them a special message.

Nan then looked over at Millie. She couldn't be sure, but it felt like something was shifting in her, too.

CHAPTER 12

# Sage Advice

When Millie begged them all to go to the big summer flea market, Nan didn't argue. She was tired of chasing the dream to save Millie's house but she didn't have the energy to fight it either. She didn't want to be blamed again for a "lack of persistence" so she kept her mouth shut but, as far as she was concerned, their fun little game of treasure hunting had turned into a relentless search for nothing.

She had complained to her mom, thinking she'd get at least a little sympathy, but Ms. Webster told her she needed to change her perspective. Sometimes her mom could be so unrealistic.

When they arrived at the Broad Street Fair Grounds, Nan found it to be even more than she had imagined it would be…more hot, more crowded, and more old junk. She was sick of being around old things. Everything in her life felt old and worn out…her clothes, her home, her summer, even her thoughts. They all felt old. She was tired of feeling like she'd never have anything more.

Feeling grumpier by the minute, she was relieved when they agreed to split up and "look for treasure" separately. For once, she didn't mind being the one to look after Kara and was content to let Kara decide where to go. For whatever reason, Chubbs was also content to follow Kara, waddling at her heels.

Thankfully for Nan, Kara led them into the shade of a large tent, its tarp sides strangely flapping against the supporting poles even though there was no breeze.

Kara made her way to the back corner of the tent and planted herself in front of a long table.

As Nan's eyes adjusted to the dim light, she saw what must have attracted her sister: beautiful flowers, stars, unicorns, fairies, all painted in brilliant colors on rocks of different shapes and sizes. Perfect for a little rock collector and her magic rock-finding pig!

There was an old woman sitting on a squeaky old rocking chair behind the table, fanning herself with a small piece of cardboard. The woman leaned forward and squinted at Kara. She had a wrinkly face and crooked fingers. Her dress was so faded it was difficult to tell what color it had been when it was new. The white apron she wore over it was covered with streaks of paint. Perched atop her head was a floppy straw hat with a purple ribbon threaded around the brim.

If the old woman noticed Nan, she didn't let on. All her attention was focused on Kara. And if Nan found the woman to be a little scary, Kara didn't seem at all wary.

"What do you think of my pretties?" the woman asked Kara, in a hoarse whisper.

"They're beautiful!" Kara exclaimed. "Did you make them?"

"I did," she answered, and swept her arms in a big circle around her. "With a little help from my friends," she added.

Nan looked around to see what friends she was talking about, but there was no one else anywhere around.

The old woman picked up a plain rock and held it up to one eye, looking it over carefully. Nan wondered if she might be blind in the other one.

"Which one do you desire?" the old woman asked. Kara walked up and back, looking at individual rocks but not touching even one. Chubbs plopped down on the cool pavement and panted like the part-dog he seemed to be.

"Well," Kara finally answered, "I only collect rocks with writing on them."

"You don't say," the woman murmured. "And what kind of writing do your rocks have on them?"

Kara put her hands on her hips and tapped her foot, looking an awful lot like their mom and with an attitude to match! "I have desire and faith," she began confidently, "and things and thoughts, and imagination." She shifted her hips. "I have more but I can't remember them all right now."

Nan almost laughed out loud. She was impressed that Kara had remembered so many of the words and was acting so big, especially in front of someone she didn't even know!

The old woman looked at Nan for the first time, peering up at her over her spectacles. Nan shifted uncomfortably as the woman held her gaze for one drawn-out moment.

The woman sat back in her chair and closed her eyes. She rocked back and forth a few times and then stopped abruptly. Something about the woman's behavior made Nan feel a little nervous. She looked around but they were still the only ones in the tent.

Kara put her elbows on the table, leaning closer to the strange old woman. Nan reached for Kara's hand, thinking that they should probably go. No sooner did she have that thought when, suddenly, the old woman sat up and snapped her fingers. The girls jumped back! Chubbs lifted his head.

The woman looked at Kara intently and pointed at her with a shaky finger. "I know just the thing," she said. Her voice seemed even more crackly than before.

Nan watched as she bent down awkwardly and brought up a wooden tray from behind the table. Sitting on it were baby food jars full of paint. She scooted herself and the chair closer to the table.

"So," she began, "you already have desire, you say." She picked up the rock she had inspected before and then a paintbrush. She dipped the brush in the jar of red paint and began painting on the rock with small dabs. "Desire is the seed you need," she said, "and so it begins."

She dipped the brush in water, swirled it around, and then wiped it on her apron. It left a faint streak of red to blend in with the rest of the colors.

"Faith is like the sun," she said as she dipped into another color. "Let's make it a big purple one." Again, she cleaned the brush just as she had before, swirling and wiping.

"Now, some imagination. I'll use swirls of pink, don't you think?"

Kara stood trance-like, nodding her head every time the old woman spoke.

Nan also found herself to be strangely captivated by all the dipping and painting and chanting.

"The power is in the seed, not the flower," continued the woman. "Do you know when the seed will grow?"

Kara spoke almost before the woman had finished the question. "Seeds have to decide to grow or they'll just sit in the ground forever," she said.

"Smart little girl you are," she said. "So you must know what makes the seed decide."

At this point, the woman's hand was moving so quickly from jar to jar, Nan couldn't tell if she was painting the rock or just moving her hand. If she believed in such nonsense, she might have thought the old woman was casting a spell on the rock.

"Of course, it's love! Love from above. It's in the air and in the ground, tending the seed, the seed in need."

The old woman stopped to look at Nan for one quick moment then dipped her brush in blue. "Some blue," she said, "so the good thoughts can come through."

Finally, the woman held up the rock and blew on it. She reached for a salt shaker and shook it over the rock. Glitter went everywhere. The old woman coughed.

"Hold out your hand," she said to Kara, who eagerly held out her hand without hesitation.

The old woman squinted and pursed her lips, then placed the rock into Kara's palm and closed her fingers around it. Kara began to unclasp her fingers.

"Ah-ah-ah." The old woman shook her head and wagged her finger. "You wait and look at it in the sunshine."

"But..." Kara stammered. "I don't have any money to buy this." The woman gasped. "No money? I suppose you spent it all on candy, or maybe on toys?"

"Oh, no!" Kara protested. "I gave all my money to Millie this morning."

"Gave it away, did you? Do you always give your money away?"

"No," Kara answered. "But Millie really needs it."

"I see," crackled the old woman. She sat back in her chair and began slowly rocking again.

Nan's heart sank when she saw Kara hand the rock back to the woman. She reached into her pocket for her own money but stopped when the woman continued talking.

"No, no, no," the woman said. "I painted that rock just for you. I couldn't sell it to anyone else anyway. You have to keep it now."

"Oh, thank you!" Kara exclaimed, and ran out of the tent. Chubbs lumbered behind her.

Just as Nan turned to follow Kara, she heard the old woman's hoarse whisper.

"The message is for you, too, big sister."

* * * * *

Kara held out her hand to reveal a bright, colorful rock with dazzling pink sparkles.

"Wow, that is really cool," Ace said, sincerely. "Some old lady just gave it to you?"

"She painted it just for me!"

"You can't believe how fast she did it," added Nan. "It was actually a little spooky."

"I think she's a witch," said Kara. "A good witch not a bad witch."

Millie tried to look unimpressed, but Nan could tell she was just as drawn to the beautiful rock as the rest of them were.

Kara handed the rock to Ace.

"Read it now!" she demanded sweetly.

"Okay, okay!" said Ace, with a warm smile.

## – Tend to Your Subconscious Mind –

Kara reached up to take the rock back. "It's my magic garden rock!" she said, excitedly. She held it up for Jack to see. "See that seed? Love is making it grow!" she exclaimed.

"Why would someone write that for a five-year-old kid?!" Millie exclaimed. "How would she even know what a subconscious mind is? That's just stupid."

Kara turned to look straight at Millie. "It's not stupid!"

Nan jumped in. "No, Kara, it's really special. It doesn't even really matter what it says. It's really beautiful."

Nan remembered what the woman had said, that the message was for her, too. She mulled the words over to herself and tried to remember what the old woman had said while she was painting it.

"Can I see that again, Kara?" Jack asked. Kara handed the rock to Jack who examined it more closely. "I wonder what kind of rock this is. I've never seen anything like it."

"Who cares?!" Millie growled and snatched the rock. "It's a rock with paint all over it!"

"Hey, give that back!" Kara cried.

"Come on, Millie," Ace said. "Don't start that again."

Millie stomped her foot and shoved the rock back into Kara's outstretched palm. "Here!" she huffed.

"We're all just hot and tired, you guys," Jack inserted.

"And thirsty," said Nan.

"I'm thirsty, too," said Kara.

At that exact moment, an old man appeared with a cooler strapped on his hip, filled with ice and water bottles. A handmade sign hung around his neck. It said "50 cents".

"You kids here need some water?" he asked, with a creaky southern accent.

"Wow, yeah," said Ace, handing him a dollar. "Our thoughts must have been really powerful! How about some ice cream, too?"

"I want ice cream," said Kara, hopefully.

"Sorry, young one," the man said, giving Kara a soft pat on the head, "I only have water today."

Jack bought three more bottles of water and gave them to the girls.

"Now, that's a nice rock you have there," he said. "May I take a look?"

Kara held up her rock for him to see, but wasn't about to let it go.

"That sure looks magical to me."

Kara nodded.

"The garden of your mind," he repeated slowly. "We don't know the half of what is growin' in there! Do you know people say we only use about ten percent of these brains?" he asked, knocking on his head.

The old man unhooked the cooler from around his waist and put it on the ground. "All those thoughts in there! Most of them are takin' up residence in your subconscious mind, growin' whether you want them to or not!" he said.

Nan looked at her friends, hoping to make a graceful exit, but no one met her glance. They all seemed content to stand there for the moment and listen to the funny old man, even Millie. Nan had to admit the man *was* a little captivating.

"Them bad thoughts, negative thoughts, ugly thoughts," he said, looking back and forth between Nan and Millie, "if you don't pull 'em out early, they'll grow like weeds, I tell ya."

Nan wondered why he was looking at her. Did he think she had a head full of negative, ugly thoughts? She hoped not.

The man continued with more enthusiasm. "You gotta get in there and yank them things out! Yank 'em out before they become hard-fast beliefs, I say. Those beliefs will keep you down and keep you from seein' the opportunities that are sittin' right in front of your face."

He bent down and gestured for the kids to come in a little closer. Nan shifted uncomfortably while the others moved in.

"Now, herein lies the secret," he said a little softer. "You get that mind of yours all fertile, like a field ready for plantin'. And then you drop in thoughts of the things you want more than anythin' else in this here world. Them things will start a-growin', you can bet they will. You water 'em with faith and love and thanks and see what comes up.

"But listen up. You gotta let go of how you think things will turn out, 'cause it's not up to you. You plant your intentions and then you trust that you'll get exactly what you need, even if you might not recognize it right off the bat."

The old man bent down to pick up his cooler and looked up at them. Nan thought he was looking straight at her. "That's all I gotta say about that," he said, and then gave Kara another pat on the head. "That's a good rock you have," he reassured her, and walked away.

Nan wasn't sure if the old man had confused everyone else, but she thought he was a little crazy. "He sure had a lot to say about nothing," she said, and then regretted opening her mouth at all.

"I liked him," said Millie. "I think he's a wise old man."

Nan looked at Millie, wondering what had come over her.

"Me, too," said Kara. "He told a funny story!"

"He sure made some good sense of Kara's rock," said Jack.

"Yep, made sense to me," agreed Ace, much to Nan's surprise.

She felt weird. Ace was agreeing with Jack, Millie was suddenly being nice, and all Nan could feel was annoyed. Maybe she was just a head full of negative thoughts, she thought disgustedly.

"I want a popsicle," said Kara.

"No," said Nan, curtly. "It's time to go."

As they all walked toward the bus stop, Kara pulled on Nan's arm.

"What?" she demanded impatiently.

Kara merely pointed in the direction of a nearby dumpster. Behind it, the old man they had been talking to was helping the "rock lady" into a battered old car. He looked at them…at least Nan thought he did…and winked.

"Maybe they're *both* witches," said Kara.

"I doubt it," said Nan.

CHAPTER 13

# All is Lost

The sun sizzled on the hard blacktop of the still and quiet schoolyard. Nan and Millie sat dejectedly, swaying slowly on the swings, while Jack and Ace halfheartedly kicked a soccer ball back and forth. Jack's mother had grown tired of having them in the house while she was trying to clean and had finally told them to go for a walk. The group had wandered aimlessly around the neighborhood for a bit before ending up at their grade school where Kara would be attending Kindergarten in a few weeks.

"I can't believe it's almost time to go back to school already," Nan complained. "We've hardly done anything this summer."

"I suppose you think that's my fault!" Millie snapped.

"I didn't say that!" Nan snapped back. "I just..."

Ace stopped kicking the ball long enough to roll his eyes at them. "Oh, would you two give it up already?"

"Yeah, you two spend so much time arguing," Jack moaned. He kicked the soccer ball wildly toward Ace, smacking him right in the head with it.

"Hey, watch it, you moron!"

"I didn't mean to!"

"Okay, boys!" Millie mimicked Ace. "Give it up already!"

"Shut up, Millie! I'm so tired of you!" he spat, as he turned to walk across the playground to join Kara and Chubbs in the sandbox.

"Fine, just walk away, Ace Emerson!" Millie hollered. "No one ever asked you to hang out with us anyway!"

"Leave him alone, Millie!" Nan said, jumping out of her swing and taking a stand. "After all we've been through for you, I can't believe you're so clueless."

Millie turned her evil eye on Jack, who seemed to wither beneath her gaze. "Well, aren't you gonna say something?"

"What... I..." Jack looked bewildered.

"Go, on!" Millie yelled at him. "You might as well abandon me, too! I can tell you want to!"

Jack looked at her in astonishment. "Millie! You're my best friend! You have to stop looking at everyone as the enemy. We've ALL stuck by you this summer."

"And Jack more than anyone," said Nan. She couldn't help herself.

"Just go away," Millie said, as the tears began to well up. "I..."

Before she could finish, she was interrupted by a piercing squeal.

Jack jumped up. "Let's go!" he called.

Jack and Nan ran to the sandbox, with Millie following behind. When they arrived, Kara was pulling Chubbs by his collar.

"Chubbs, stop it!" Kara begged. "Stop, you're gonna ruin the whole sandbox!"

"Chubbs!" Jack yelled. "Kara, what's going on?"

"Kara, let go of him now!" Nan yelled. Chubbs was digging furiously without regard for the fact that tiny little Kara hung from his swinging collar.

Kara was near tears. "He won't stop digging! He's tearing the whole sandbox up!"

Chubbs had his nose about a foot into the ground already and was snuffling about, squealing as he went. He had dug below the sand now, and was tossing up chunks of dirt.

"Chubbs, come on!" Ace grunted, trying to pull the gigantic pig out of the hole that he was so intent on digging.

"Come...on...Chubbs!" grunted Jack. Sweat beaded on his brow, but the pig refused to be budged. The two boys finally gave up and just stood back and watched, along with the girls.

"What do you think he's doing?" Nan asked in wonder.

"Looks like he's trying to dig his way to China," Millie joked meekly.

After a few more minutes, Chubbs suddenly stopped digging and shook the sand and dirt from his snout. His belly jiggled beneath him, and he plopped down in the sand, rolling over to scratch his back in the dirt with stumpy legs flailing in the air. Finally, he rolled back to his feet and lumbered away from the sandbox to stand in the grass and snuffle around in the shade.

Nan, Millie, Ace, and Jack all glanced at each other quickly before running to look into the deep hole that Chubbs had dug in the sandbox. They stood in a circle, looking down into the opening. Kara squeezed between their legs, crawling on her hands and knees until she was at the very edge of the hole. She lay on her stomach and poked her arms into the hole.

"There's a rock in here!" she yelled, excitedly.

"Let me see!" Millie knelt down next to Kara and reached down into the hole. "There *is* a rock. I can feel it."

"Chubbs is a magic rock-finder," squealed Kara. "He's a magic pig!"

The other three dropped to the ground next to her and began a shoving match, trying to get into the hole.

"Move it, Jack!" ordered Ace, shoving his way into the hole. After a moment, he finally wrenched the rock free and pulled it up into the sunlight. He held the rock against his chest and wiped it off on his shirt.

"There's writing on it!" Kara was the first to notice the lettering on the otherwise ordinary stone.

Nan rolled her eyes. "Of course there is…"

"Of course there is," Millie repeated.

"Read it, read it!" Kara pleaded.

Ace looked up at her, grinning. "I can't believe this! It's crazy!" He looked back down at the rock in his hands and read what it said.

– Tune Your Brain –

"Okay boys, which one of you wants to tell us how this fits in with the others?" Millie asked smugly.

Jack went first. "This is great! It's perfect! It's another metaphor for changing your thoughts," he said.

Nan thought Jack was so cute in his excitement.

"Go on," said Millie.

"Think of your brain as a radio. The radio gets all these signals coming into it, right?"

Ace joined in with enthusiasm. "You got your rock, your country, your boring old elevator music," he said.

"You have to turn on your radio in order to get the signals in the first place," said Jack. "And then choose the station you're going to listen to."

"Right," said Ace. "You can listen to rock, or country, or boring old elevator music!"

Nan smiled as Ace's sense of humor continued to grow on her.

"If your thoughts are like stations, then you can choose to tune into the good ones!" said Jack.

"And," added Ace, looking at both Millie and Nan, "if you turn your radio off, you stop receiving any signals at all. Come on, girls, open your mind and start receiving the right signals!" said Ace. He put his hands behind his head with his fingers sticking up like antennae, being goofy and making them giggle.

"Right!" Jack agreed. "We were all too busy hanging out around the swings arguing with each other. We shut off our minds, so of course we couldn't think of anything. We gotta tune our brains to the right station!"

Kara joined in, imitating Ace and making a silly face. "I'm a radio, too."

"We still have plenty of time to find the treasure," Jack said. "School doesn't start for three more weeks, and I bet there are tons of places we haven't looked yet!"

Millie burst into tears. Somehow, she went from laughing to crying, in a matter of seconds.

"What is it, Millie?" Ace said with true concern. They had all grown used to seeing Millie pout and cry, but for some reason this time seemed oddly different. "Are you okay?"

"N-N-Noooo..." Millie sobbed.

"What happened?" Nan asked her. "We were just playing."

"It's...it's all over!" Millie cried out. "It's too late!"

Kara moved a little closer to Nan.

"What do you mean, too late?" Jack asked.

"It's no use!" Millie spat the words out, looking around helplessly at her friends. Her whole body shuttered and seemed to sink into the ground. "We have to be out of our house by the end of the month," she said.

"What are you talking about?" asked Nan. She couldn't imagine that Millie was serious, but it sure seemed that way.

"We have to stay with my grandparents in Indiana."

"Well, that can't be too bad. I love spending time with my grandparents," offered Ace.

"Stay, as in *live* with," Millie retorted.

Nan held her breath, hoping Ace would stop talking. He was obviously trying to make Millie feel better but he was making it awkwardly worse.

He seemed to get the message or realized it himself, though, because he did stop. "I'm sorry, Millie," he said sincerely. Nan put her hand on Ace's shoulder. It seemed like the right thing to do.

Millie started crying again. "And my dad's not coming with us."

Everyone started speaking all at once.

"Whoa!" exclaimed Nan.

"How can your dad not go with you?" Ace asked.

Jack was instantly sympathetic. "It's okay, Millie," he told her, even though it was obvious that he didn't believe it.

Nan felt her heart melt. Two of her friends would be living without their dads. It took a moment more before she realized that she, too, knew what that was like. She felt like crying, herself.

Kara piped in with the question no one wanted to ask. "Are your parents getting a divorce?"

Millie shook her head. "They say no," she started, "but I don't know. My dad says he can't come with us 'til he sells his business and finds a new job. But I know he doesn't want to sell his business."

She looked up but then lowered her eyes again. "And my mom keeps telling him how selfish he is. She keeps telling him he could have saved the house if he'd sold the business months ago. But then how would she expect us to live if my dad stopped working? It feels so mixed up, and my parents are fighting like crazy... I just know I'm never gonna see my dad again if we leave!"

Millie burst into tears all over again.

Nan felt an overwhelming, and totally uncharacteristic, urge to throw her arms around Millie and give her a huge heartfelt hug. No one was more surprised than Nan when she held Millie close and began to cry along with her. "I'm so sorry, Millie!"

"Me, too!" Kara threw her own arms around her older sister and Millie.

Chubbs nudged his snout in between the girls and tried to squeeze his huge body into the middle of the girls.

Jack and Ace looked at each other awkwardly. Nan was sure neither of them quite knew what to do, but was glad they stayed.

Their summer adventures may not have resulted in saving Millie's house, but it had definitely brought them all closer together and Nan liked that. She liked that a lot.

## CHAPTER 14

# Things Change

Nan and Kara walked hand in hand toward home. Nan was glad for the walk. It had been such an emotional afternoon. She felt tired, but in a good sort of way. She felt like something was changing, like something inside her was moving around and finding a new home. It wouldn't make sense if she tried to talk about it, but that's the way it felt.

Kara was dragging her feet and fumbling with her rock. Nan even had a new appreciation for her sister. She was feeling proud of her and didn't find her so annoying anymore, either.

Suddenly, and for no apparent reason, Kara stopped and threw her rock into the ditch with as much force as she could muster.

"Kara!" Nan exclaimed. "Why would you do that?"

"I don't care about those stupid rocks anymore! They're not helping Millie at all!" she said, her lower lip beginning to tremble. Nan couldn't stand it when she did that.

"I know," Nan said lovingly. She stooped down to Kara's eye level. "But, don't you think you'll regret it later if you don't bring that rock home with you?"

"I don't care, I just..."

Kara was interrupted by the sound of a honking horn, and the two girls turned to see who it was. An old blue minivan pulled up beside them, and they saw the driver through the open window.

"Mom?!" said Nan. She was shocked, absolutely shocked.

"Surprise!" Ms. Webster grinned at her daughters' astonished faces. "Hop in girls, we're goin' out to celebrate!"

"Celebrate what?" Kara asked, her mood shifting in an instant.

"Whose car is this?" Nan asked at the same time.

Ms. Webster laughed. "We are going to celebrate the fact that your mother is a genius…and, this is MY van!"

Nan was stunned. "What? What are you talking about? How can we afford a van?"

"Well, stop staring and get in! Come on, I'll tell you all about it."

Nan slid the side door of the van open and climbed in with Kara fast behind her. "I can't believe this!" she laughed. "How is this possible?" She slammed the door, and her mother began to pull away from the curb.

"Wait!" Kara exclaimed. "My rock!"

"Mom, wait!" Nan cried. "Kara left her rock by the road!"

Ms. Webster stopped the van, and Nan jumped out. She ran back to retrieve Kara's rock and returned to the van. She smiled at her sister, handing the stone to her. "I'm glad you changed your mind," she whispered. Kara smiled and held the rock close.

"So, you found another rock, huh?" their mother asked. "Good! I have a great idea about what we can do with all those rocks of yours."

"Really, what?" Kara asked.

"You'll see."

"So Mom," Nan asked, "where did the van come from? I thought we would never be able to afford a car."

"Well, technically we still can't," Ms. Webster admitted. "The van doesn't actually belong to me. Technically it belongs to the restaurant. But, seeing as how I am now the new general manager of Warner's Family Grill, and I am going to need some reliable transportation to get back and forth to work at the drop of a hat, Mr. and Mrs. Warner have been kind enough to provide me with their old van to use as a company car."

"What?" Kara asked, confused.

"*You're* the manager of the restaurant?!" Nan asked, her excitement growing by the minute.

"That's right!" Ms. Webster turned to look over her shoulder just long enough to flash her girls a silly grin before the stoplight in front of them turned green.

Nan was speechless. She couldn't remember seeing her mother this happy in all of her life. She looked about ready to burst!

"And that's not all..." Ms. Webster continued.

"What else, Mom? What else?"

"You are also looking at the proud new owner of one old, dilapidated apartment building located at 7986 North 76$^{th}$ Street!"

"What?!" Nan and Kara exclaimed in unison.

"Wait, you're joking, right?" Nan asked, suddenly doubtful. There was no possible way that her mother's ridiculous dream of buying their apartment building was actually coming true.

"It's no joke!" Ms. Webster laughed. "It's a big day, girls... a big, big day! I have managed to wrangle a promotion *and* purchase an apartment building all in one day!"

"But...I don't..." Nan could not seem to decide which piece of amazing news she wanted to know about first.

Her mother pulled into the parking lot of an expensive Italian restaurant they had all wanted to try but "couldn't afford".

"Let's go in and get settled at a table and I'll tell you all about it."

Nan and Kara followed their mother into the beautiful restaurant. On either side of the front entryway were two glass enclosures with just a few small tables in each. Ms. Webster spoke with the hostess and they were quickly ushered into one of those enclosures and seated at a sunny table next to a lush, live, potted fig tree.

The Webster girls were utterly speechless. Their mother ordered drinks for them and then leaned toward them across the table, smiling with her dark sparkly eyes. Nan thought she looked completely beautiful, as if all of her worries and wakeful nights had magically been transformed into a beautiful dreams.

"So, would you like to hear all the juicy details?" she teased them.

"YES!" Nan and Kara answered together.

"Alright then!"

Ms. Webster smiled, and jumped right in to the most incredible story Nan had ever heard.

"Let's see, where do I start?" she began, obviously enjoying her daughters' impatience. "Oh yes, at the beginning! You know that Mr. Warner has been in and out of the hospital lately with all of his heart problems, right?"

The girls nodded.

"Well, Mrs. Warner has been trying to talk him into selling the restaurant and moving down to Arizona where their daughter lives. The stress of managing the restaurant is just more than he can take now, and Mrs. Warner wants to live near her grandchildren. Of course, Mr. Warner wants to move, too, but he can't bring himself to sell the business that he worked so hard to build. He is hoping that one of his grandchildren will eventually take over the restaurant and keep it in the family.

"So, I suggested to the Warners that they consider putting me in charge of the restaurant, and they can go ahead and live in Arizona for most of the year without giving up the restaurant completely."

"Nobody knows that restaurant like you do, Mom!" said Nan.

"That was my point, exactly! So, we sat down together yesterday afternoon and discussed exactly what it was we all wanted, and we came up with a fabulous plan that works for all of us!"

"Oh my gosh, Mom! That is so awesome!"

"Can we eat there for free now?" asked Kara.

Ms. Webster smiled at her youngest and touched her cheek sweetly.

"But, what about the apartment building?" Nan asked. "I mean, what does that have to do with the restaurant?"

"Good question," Ms. Webster told her, still grinning from ear to ear. "Here's the connection. Thinking about the Warners retiring and moving to Arizona got me thinking about the owners of our building. Mrs. Gizewski has been trying to talk Mr. Gizewski into selling it for at least the last ten years. They own a beautiful house out in the country that they have been renting out forever, but you know how cheap Mr. G. is! He couldn't see the practicality of moving out of their cheap little apartment as long as they could still rent out the house and earn some extra income.

"Anyway, it's truly amazing how this all came together! Mrs. G. told me that their renters recently moved out, and I mentioned in my conversation with the Warners that this could be the perfect time for me to make my move and talk Mr. G. into selling the building to me. Making so much more money at the restaurant gives me a better chance of securing the loan I need."

"And?" Nan asked, following every word.

Just then their waitress appeared with her note pad, ready to take their orders.

"Oh, goodness," Ms. Webster said. "We didn't even get around to looking at the menus yet. This is our first time here, what would you suggest?"

Nan grew impatient while her mother discussed the menu with the waitress and finally settled on a platter with three separate dishes. Another server appeared at the table with a basket of bread and a dish of oil with herbs floating around the bottom of the dish.

"What's that?" Kara asked.

"That's olive oil with balsamic vinegar," Ms. Webster answered, pulling a piece of bread from the loaf and handing it to Kara. She pulled another piece for Nan, and a third for herself. "See, you dip your bread in it and then eat it." She closed her eyes and sighed. "Oh, this is so good!"

Kara followed her mother's example and dipped her own bread into the olive oil mixture. Nan held her piece of bread and just stared at her mother.

"Mmm, try it Nan!" Kara told her. "It's yummy!"

"Mom, go on! What about the apartment building?" Nan prodded. She was not about to try anything until her mother continued her story.

Ms. Webster dabbed at her lips with her cloth napkin.

Nan rolled her eyes. Her mom loved to drag things out.

"Mmm..." hummed Ms. Webster, clearly enjoying the bread, and the moment!

"Mo-om!"

"Well, the Warners have known forever that I've wanted to purchase our building..."

"Who *doesn't* know?" joked Nan. She finally took a bite of the bread that Kara was quickly devouring on her own.

"*And*," her mom continued, "I just happened to mention that this might be a good time for me to jump on it. It didn't even occur to me that they would jump in and offer to help me."

Ms. Webster let this last piece of information linger for effect.

"The Warners are helping you buy the apartment building?" Nan asked, stunned again. "Why would they want to do that?"

"Yes!" said Ms. Webster, laughing with delight. "The Warners have offered to co-sign the loan for the apartment building! They're also providing the down payment, which makes it a whole lot easier for me."

"So, they're just gonna give you the money?!" Nan asked in astonishment.

"No, no, no Nan," said her mother, shaking her head. "Of course they're not going to just give me the money. The Warners are nice people, but they're not foolish! They're going to be, what we call, silent partners...for now, anyway. They'll earn a small percentage of the profits until I can afford to buy them out."

All the financial lingo left Nan feeling a bit confused. "But, you do actually own the building?" she asked.

"Yep." Ms. Webster was grinning once more. "The building is ours!"

"But how did it happen so fast?" asked Nan.

"Sweetie," said Ms. Webster, "I've been working on this for years. When everything came together in this big, beautiful opportunity, I was ready for it. Thank goodness, I was ready for it!"

Nan watched her mom's eyes fill up with tears.

Ms. Webster reached across the table and squeezed both her girls' hands. "We are so fortunate, girls. And I'm so happy to share this with you, my amazing daughters!"

Nan was flooded with emotion and her eyes welled up, too.

The waitress approached with a huge tray holding a platter full of steaming and bubbling food. It smelled delicious.

"And just look at this spread!" said Ms. Webster.

Ms. Webster grabbed a large spoon and began to fill their plates from the platter as the waitress left them to enjoy their dinner. "Can you believe we are actually eating here?" Ms. Webster asked.

Their own mouths were already too full for either of them to answer, so they simply shook their heads and ate in silence for a few minutes. After a while, Kara stopped eating and stared into her plate, twirling her fork in her linguini and staring at it as it spiraled up the utensil.

"Okay, you, what's the matter?" Ms. Webster asked sternly. "Why the long face? Are you worried about something?"

"I'm sad that Millie's moving away," Kara said.

Nan wished Kara hadn't said anything. She didn't want one little thing to ruin what was probably the biggest day of her mom's life.

"Really?" Ms. Webster asked, confused. "I didn't think you girls really liked Millie. Are you going to miss her that much?"

"It's not just that…" Nan said.

Kara spoke up. "Millie's going to live with her grandma, and her daddy's not even going."

"Oh?" Ms. Webster replied. "Are Millie's parents getting a divorce?"

"They say they're not," said Nan, "but Millie says they've been fighting a lot, and she doesn't think her dad is going to go live with them."

"I see," Ms. Webster said, giving them her full attention.

"We tried to find a treasure to save their house, but now it's too late, and Millie's gonna be homeless if they don't go live with her grandma," Kara mumbled her last few words through a mouth full of chicken Parmesan. "Ow!" she cried out, as Nan kicked her under the table.

It just sounded so silly that they had wasted their entire summer on a ridiculous treasure hunt.

"Homeless?" Ms. Webster asked. "I can't quite believe that. I thought the Medlins were doing really well. Nan, do you know what's going on?"

Nan looked at her mother for a moment before breaking down and explaining the whole situation. She actually felt relieved as she unloaded every detail, telling her all about the treasure, even Millie's attitude about credit cards. When she finally finished, she wondered why she hadn't told her mother everything before. It felt really good to share it all.

"Hmm..." Ms. Webster thought for a moment. "Why don't you girls let me worry about the Medlins. Maybe there's something I can do to help them."

"Really?" Kara asked hopefully.

Nan felt doubtful as usual, but decided to have faith in her mother who really did seem to know what she was doing after all.

"Absolutely," Ms. Webster reassured her daughters. "This is a grown-up issue, and you should let us grown-ups figure it out. I wish you would have told me about this earlier."

Nan and Kara glanced at each other.

"Don't worry," she told them, "not right now, anyway."

Ms. Webster took hold of both her daughters' hands lovingly. "Who has room for dessert?"

CHAPTER 15

# Millie's Makeover

Nan watched quietly while Millie sorted through her closet, picking out items to sell at the neighborhood rummage sale. Mrs. Emerson had taken it upon herself to help the Medlins "pare down" their many belongings as they prepared to move. Nan thought it must have taken a lot of convincing for Millie's mom to agree. Mrs. Medlin was not one to look less than perfect in public.

Kara sat in the middle of Millie's huge, wraparound doll house, playing with a collection of expensive dolls that looked like they had just come out of their boxes.

The melodic chiming of the doorbell echoed through the enormous house, and a few minutes later, Mr. Medlin called up the stairs to his daughter. "Millie, girls, Jack and Ace are here."

Millie barely glanced up from her gloomy task, so Nan went to the bedroom door and poked her head into the hall. She was more than surprised when Jack and Ace appeared at the top of the massive staircase with Chubbs lumbering nimbly behind them.

"Oh…my…gosh!" she exclaimed. "I cannot believe Mr. Medlin let you bring him up here!"

Jack flashed a self-satisfied grin, but quickly sobered when he saw the pout on Millie's face. "Is it okay if Chubbs comes into your room?" he asked politely.

Millie only shrugged. "That's fine," she said, and continued going through the extensive collection of clothes inside her closet.

Nan felt like she was in a time warp. Here was Chubbs, in Millie's room, and Millie was barely taking notice.

The others seemed to be just as baffled as they stood quietly before she finally spoke.

"You know, I haven't even worn half this stuff," Millie admitted.

"Really?" Nan asked, even though she had already assumed as much. She couldn't imagine having all of those wonderful clothes and never bothering to wear them. If she had Millie's wardrobe, she could wear a different outfit every day of the year.

Suddenly, Millie grabbed an arm load of clothing and yanked it all out of the closet, then tossed it into an open box on the floor. Nan and Kara both gasped in disbelief.

"What are you doing?" Ace asked. "You can't give all of your clothes away!"

"I'm not giving them away," Millie corrected him. "I'm selling them. I don't wear any of this stuff anyway. I've been standing here thinking that I have five favorite outfits that I wear all the time, and the rest just hangs here making my closet look pretty. What's the point?"

Nan could not believe what she was hearing.

Chubbs began to nose around in the box. Jack quickly grabbed him by his collar, pulling him away.

The fat pig redirected his short attention span to Kara, leaning slightly against her, begging to have his ears scratched. Millie shook her head and laughed at him. The others were speechless.

"What?" Millie asked. "Why are you looking at me like that?"

"Um, nothing," Ace mumbled. "No reason. Do you need any help?"

Nan smiled as she watched Ace. She noticed how his eyes got a little squinty when he got embarrassed and thought it was cute.

Millie glanced around her room and seemed to despair at the huge amount of *things* that had to be packed up. She seemed to come to a decision, though, and told the others, "How about we do this…I will go through each section and just pack what I want to keep, and you can start throwing everything else in those boxes and take them down to the garage. I'm not gonna have much room at my grandma's house, so there's no point trying to keep any of this if my parents can sell it and get some extra money."

Millie carefully picked out a small pile of clothes from what remained in her closet and packed them into her pink designer suitcase. She moved on to her toys, while Nan began to pack the rest of the clothes into boxes.

"Nan, you can have some of those clothes if any of them fit you," Millie said over her shoulder before turning her attention to Kara.

Nan stopped and stared at Millie in surprise.

"Kara, do you want to take a couple of these dolls?" Millie continued.

Kara's eyes lit up. "Yeah!"

"Gosh, thanks, Millie," Nan said quietly, appreciating Millie's change in attitude and also hoping it wouldn't suddenly change back.

Jack began to disassemble the huge doll house that had gotten so little use. Nan remembered hearing about how Millie had begged for it for her birthday.

Millie opened the door to a large mahogany box, which was almost as tall as she was. She dug through it, seemingly looking for something in particular. Chubbs nosed her elbow, trying to see what she was doing.

"Stop it, you stupid pig," said Millie, but with no particular emotion.

An irritated look crossed Jack's face, but Ace shook his head at him in warning, and Jack went back to packing up Millie's toys. It seemed as if no one wanted to break the spell on Millie!

"Oh, here it is," Millie said finally. "My grandma gave me this bracelet right before she died...my dad's mom, not my mom's mom who we're going to live with." Millie sighed. "I really miss her."

Millie put the bracelet on and held it up so it sparkled in a stream of sunlight. "This is the only piece of jewelry I have that's worth keeping. The rest is just junk."

Nan gave her a puzzled look. "What about that huge diamond necklace you got last year? I thought you said it was worth $10,000."

Nan remembered the huge bauble that Millie had flashed around school for a month.

Millie just blushed and glanced down at Chubbs, who was nosing through her jewelry. "Hey, get out of there!" she exclaimed in an attempt to get Chubbs' attention. She moved swiftly toward the pig, trying to shove him aside, but the two of them ended up crashing into the jewelry box together, breaking off one of its wooden legs and falling into a wild, squealing pile on the shiny hardwood floor.

"Chubbs!" Jack exclaimed, running to try to pull his beloved pet from the mess. Chubbs threw his head into the case, somehow managing to get tangled up in several beaded necklaces that hung inside. Gold and jewels cascaded from the tangle.

"Wow, look at all that treasure!" Kara exclaimed. "Millie, you had a treasure here in your house all along!"

Ace snorted loudly, obviously trying not to laugh. As soon as Nan looked at Ace, though, she couldn't keep it in and, soon, they were all laughing together. Even Millie, who was visibly relieved at the tension breaker that Chubbs had created, joined in.

Once again, Millie stunned Nan by throwing her arms around Chubbs in a loving embrace. Just as suddenly, though, she seemed to realize what she had just done and looked up in embarrassment.

"Okay, fine," she told them. "So, the stupid pig is starting to grow on me. Is that a crime?"

"No!" Jack told her. "I'm glad he's growing on you. I knew he would if you just gave him a chance."

Ace finally calmed down enough to offer Millie a hand. She stood up and surveyed the mess in the midst of her elegantly decorated room. Finally, she looked at Nan and then at Kara. She stooped down to pick up a handful of sparkly jewels and tossed them lightly toward them both.

"Here, have some!" she called to them, giggling at the surprised looks on their faces. The jewels fell over them both, sunlight sparkling all over the walls.

Nan thought Millie's walls made a wonderful ballroom!

"Oh, don't look so surprised!" Millie laughed. "They're just glass." A thoughtful look crossed her face, and she turned and began digging in her messy jewelry box again. Finally finding what she was looking for, she pulled out the huge diamond that Nan had just questioned her about and held it up in triumph.

Kara gazed at the rock in awe. Sunlight continued to pour through the huge, sunny window, concentrating its rays into the spectacular diamond before pouring back out in a colorful rainbow that filled the room. Kara's eyes nearly popped out of her head when Millie extended her hand, offering the rock to her.

"This is for you," Millie stated simply.

Kara seemed to be frozen in place. Nan could not believe that Millie was actually offering this massive, expensive diamond to her little sister.

"Go on, take it," Millie urged her.

Kara reached out tentatively, maybe expecting Millie to snatch the rock back at the last second.

Nan watched her as she closed her little fingers around the diamond, and held it close against her chest, eyes shining with happiness.

"Millie," Nan scolded, shaking her head. "Have you lost your mind? You can't give Kara a real diamond like that! Don't you think your parents will want to sell it?"

Millie shook her head and laughed, enjoying the reaction she had incited in her friends. "That diamond isn't real either," she said, "and I want Kara to have it for her collection. It will do her a lot more good than it has me."

"So, you lied?" Nan asked.

"Well…" Millie said, "I didn't ever lie, really. I only said it *could be* worth $10,000. And it could, if it were a real diamond."

Nan felt a sudden twinge of sadness. Maybe she had made things up about Millie to make it easier to dislike her. She felt sorry for being jealous of Millie for reasons that didn't seem to matter anymore.

"Oh my gosh!" said Millie. "I just remembered!" She went back into her closet and came out with a plain wooden jewelry box that was made to look like a miniature door. "This goes with the diamond," she exclaimed. "And, look, Kara! It has writing on it!"

Kara's eyes lit up again as Millie opened up the box and held it up for all to see.

The box was lined in red velvet and had an indentation in the middle that was the same shape as the diamond. Kara placed the gemstone in its place.

"Here, look," said Millie, closing the lid.

The inscription was centered on the box, in beautiful cursive lettering. Millie read aloud what it said.

– Open the Door to the 6th Sense –

"I don't know what that means," said Kara.

"Doesn't the 6th sense have something to do with psychics and stuff?" Ace asked. "I don't believe in all that garbage."

"Me, neither," Jack added. "Psychics are a bunch of scammers."

Millie rolled her eyes at the boys and sat down next to Kara. She spoke to her in a whisper, and Nan had to lean forward to hear her. "Don't listen to them, Kara. My grandma told me all about the 6th Sense when she gave this to me. I didn't really get it then, but I think I understand it now.

"The 6th Sense is something we all have, whether we know it or not. It's like your instincts, or like when you get a hunch about something. It's when you just know something without knowing how you know it. Do you know what I'm talking about?"

Kara nodded as if she were in a trance.

Nan could feel her heart melting even more as she watched how sweetly Millie was talking to Kara. She had never seen her like this.

Millie went on. "Kara, I think that the door is right in here." Millie tapped on Kara's chest. "My grandma tried to tell me that, I think."

Nan and the boys remained quiet, allowing Millie and Kara to have their sweet moment together.

"You know, it's so strange," said Millie, as she leaned back on her arms, "when I stood there and looked into my closet just now, I realized how stupid it was that I had so many clothes I don't even wear, and that's part of why we're losing our house. How could I be so dumb?"

Nan was amazed at the transformation she was seeing take place in Millie right before her eyes. She felt a shiver go up her back, and the skin on her arms tingled as if someone had lightly brushed them with a feather.

The doorbell rang for the second time since Nan had arrived that morning, and she was surprised to hear her own mother's voice drifting up from the ground floor.

Millie looked at Nan with a puzzled look on her face. "Is that your mom?"

"Yeah, I wonder what she's doing here."

Nan didn't think her mother had ever been to the Medlin home. Ms. Webster had gone to high school with both Mrs. Medlin and Mrs. Emerson, but they had never really been friends. Not that they were enemies, either, but they led such different lives, they just never seemed to have anything to say to each other.

Nan and Millie slipped out into the hall, and the others followed. They put their heads through the banister at the top of the stairs and tried to hear what was being said down below.

"Do we have to go home now?" Kara asked loudly.

"Sshh!" Millie and Nan shushed Kara together and glanced at each other. Something was up but it wasn't about having to go home. Nan could just feel it. She couldn't say how, but she just knew that something was about to happen. Her 6th sense was on high alert!

"Let's step into the study," they heard Mr. Medlin say, and then silence.

CHAPTER 16

# New Neighbors

They were all pretty quiet at dinner that night, and Nan only picked at her food. She couldn't stop thinking about the change in Millie, or why her mom had come to Millie's. Maybe there had been some kind of trouble after all. Maybe there was something worse going on, like Millie had a horrible disease or something. Nan blew at the candle her mom had lit. The flame flickered.

"What's wrong, Nan?" Ms. Webster asked. "I thought you liked my pork chops?"

Nan glanced up, called back to the table from the far away place her mind had gone. "No, the pork chops are fine," she said, taking a big bite and chewing with forced enthusiasm.

"Why does Millie have to move away?" Kara asked suddenly. "And she has to get rid of all of her stuff."

"Life doesn't always seem fair, does it?" her mother said gently. "But, I think it's probably a good thing. No one on this earth needs that much stuff, especially if the stuff causes financial problems in your life. It's completely out of balance."

"That's just what Millie said," Nan added, while chewing.

"Oh, did she?"

Nan swallowed and continued. "Yeah, she said it suddenly occurred to her that it was stupid for her parents to lose their house just so they could fill her closet up with stuff she's never even used."

"Sounds like Millie has more sense than I gave her credit for."

Nan nodded in agreement.

"But, it's still not fair she has to move away," Kara pouted. "We'll never get to see her again."

Ms. Webster smiled at them with that twinkle in her eye. "Well, then, I guess you won't be too disappointed if Millie and her parents move down the hall from us."

Kara squealed with excitement, but Nan was confused.

"What?" Nan asked. "What do you mean? How's that going to work if they don't have any money? We can't afford to just let them live here for free, can we?"

"Oh, they're not going to live here for free," Ms. Webster assured her daughter. "But I love that you're already saying 'we' and taking some ownership."

Nan gave her mom a silly smile. She was beginning to get that giddy feeling again!

Ms. Webster went on to reveal what Nan thought was simply an ingenious plan.

"Mr. Medlin is going to redo the wiring throughout the entire building in exchange for rent. That way, he can still keep his contracting business and work here around his other jobs. And that saves me money, too!"

"Wow," was just about all Nan could say.

Her mom had thought it all through. It was like she had been creating magic for everyone they knew! Nan thought back to all the late nights, the research, and all the crazy dreams. It was her mom's way of believing, having faith, making plans, working with other people, and never giving up! Nan's mind was reeling. "Wow," she said again.

Ms. Webster still wasn't done telling them all the news. "Mrs. Medlin is going to come work at the restaurant, too." She took a bite of her mashed potatoes and paused for effect, which worked like a charm on Nan.

"No, she is not!" exclaimed Nan in total disbelief. She rolled her eyes at the ridiculous idea of Mrs. Medlin working anywhere, let alone a restaurant. She was sure that type of work was beneath Millie's snobby mother.

"Oh, yes she is."

"Doing what? Washing dishes?" Nan ranted. "I doubt it!"

"No," Ms. Webster informed her daughter. "She is going to be working as a hostess. She'll greet the customers at the door and take them to their tables. I think she is an excellent choice."

Nan was still skeptical. "If you say so."

Kara giggled.

"See, even Kara doesn't believe you!" said Nan.

"I'm serious, you two," Ms. Webster said. "You can laugh if you want, but just think about it for a moment. Mrs. Medlin will be the very first person our customers see when they walk in. She might even class up the joint a bit. And it's a huge opportunity for her to appreciate the money she's earning herself as opposed to just spending money that came from someone else's hard work, or simply pulling out a credit card."

"I guess." Nan still wasn't sure if she believed her mother. "I bet Millie won't be too happy about that."

"Why do you say that?"

"How embarrassing to have her mom working at Warner's Family Grill," Nan said. Nan almost choked. As soon as the words spilled out of her mouth, she realized what she had said.

"Nan," said Ms. Webster, looking pointedly at her daughter.

Nan felt sick.

"Mom," she began. "I didn't mean...I don't mean..." She couldn't find the words to tell her mom that she couldn't be more sorry for what she had just said. She had nothing but tears.

"Nan," said her mom again. "I understand, honey. I really do. Come here."

Ms. Webster dragged Nan onto her lap and held her close. Nan couldn't believe that her mom wasn't angry or hurt. What she had said was just awful.

"I know it's been hard for you girls. Don't think I don't know that." She took Nan's chin in her hand and looked her square in the face. "And just what kind of a mom would I be if I didn't embarrass my daughters once in a while?" she joked, lovingly. "Sweetie, I want you to have compassion for Millie, and her parents."

Nan hugged her mom and slid back into her own chair.

"We all fall down in our lives. It doesn't make you a failure. Even falling down a hundred times, or a million times still doesn't make you a failure. My dad, your grandpa always said, 'Most people don't plan to fail; they fail to plan.'"

Nan was surprised to hear her mom mention her grandfather. They didn't usually talk about the past.

Ms. Webster went on. "You know, whenever you fail at a task, there are two things you can do. You can give up and go on being a failure for the rest of your life or you can take a long, hard look at yourself and figure out what went wrong. You can learn from your mistakes and vow not to repeat them. Then you get back up, dust yourself off, and move on toward your goal."

Ms. Webster paused to move the food around on her plate. She did that when she was working something out in her head. "That's not to say that you won't fail the next time, or even the time after that. But eventually, you will figure out each and every thing that could possibly go wrong, and someday, get it right. It may not be tomorrow, or next week, or even next year. But, the important thing to remember is to just keep at it. If you want something badly enough and you develop a plan to work toward it, someday it will be yours."

By this time, Kara had scooted off her chair and was playing with her new dolls on the couch. Nan, however, didn't budge. She wanted to hear everything her mom had to say.

"My plan was to buy this building and turn it into a respectable, profitable apartment complex where people are proud to live. The good, hard working tenants who have only been trying to make ends meet will have a decent place to live without having to pay more for it, and those who don't pay their rent, the ones who are always tearing their apartments up, or screaming in the halls at 2 a.m., or worse yet, trying to sell things on the front stoop...well, those people are out of here! But the important thing is this, I know I can run this place in such a way that everyone will benefit. Because I believe, if I stick to my plan and try to help others along the way, I can't help but succeed."

Ms. Webster put her head in her hands and looked at Nan. She smiled, and sighed.

"I get it, Mom. I really get it," said Nan, sincerely. "I'm sorry."

"I know, honey," said Ms. Webster, reaching for Nan's hand. "You know, maybe Millie's mom and dad can learn from the mistakes they have made and do it differently this time. Besides, the only *real* failure is the failure to participate in life to the fullest. Millie's already learning."

Nan looked at her mother with respect and admiration. She had always thought her mom was a bit loony with all of her constant dreaming, but because of her mom's planning and hard work, and her refusal to give up, she was accomplishing everything she said she would. Nan suddenly realized that the new feeling that was welling up inside her chest was pride. She was so proud of her mother she was almost bursting.

## CHAPTER 17

# Grand Re-Opening

It was the day of the grand re-opening of Rockworth Manor! Although there was still a lot of work to be done on the property, Nan's mom and Millie's dad had worked tirelessly to refurbish the lobby. They had found old photographs to use as a guide and had basically returned it to its former glory as a 1920s luxury apartment building.

For the rest of the summer and long after school began, Nan and the others had spent most of their free time helping where they could. The months passed quickly because they were all having so much fun together...way more fun than their summer treasure hunt.

Nan looked around. The lobby absolutely sparkled with new life! The old oak counter was smooth and shiny. The huge carved mirror behind the desk reminded Nan of something from a great old movie! Everything looked absolutely beautiful!

The oldest of Mrs. Davis' rowdy boys had been given his first legitimate part-time job working as one of the building's doormen, and he actually managed to look pretty good in his new uniform. Millie certainly noticed! She kept batting her eyelashes at him whenever she managed to catch his attention.

Ms. Webster paused her frantic dash around the lobby to straighten his tie and give him an encouraging wink. The other Davis boys were scrubbed, combed, and looked completely uncomfortable in their little white shirts and clip-on ties. Everything, and everybody, was transformed!

Mrs. Davis, who was now the building's Day Manager, looked ten years younger in her fresh, new dress suit. Ms. Webster had given her a rent discount so she could afford to work just one job and return to night school. Since she was working right here in the apartment building, she was able to keep a better eye on her boys, which seemed to be paying off already.

Mrs. Thompson grinned proudly over the blond heads of the squirming young lads. Nan knew she had kind of made them her pet project, hoping to make something of them after all.

The grand re-opening promised to be a well-attended affair, as Ms. Webster had managed to have the building added to the city's list of historic buildings. The local paper had run a full-page spread with pictures of the newly finished parts of the building, along with a fantastic story about the building's history. Ms. Webster had told Nan she wouldn't be surprised if she rented out most of the remaining apartments by the end of the day.

Nan, Kara, Millie, Ace, and Jack met up at the large display case that made up the front part of the main desk. Inside was Kara's rock collection. All the rocks had been polished and shined until they gleamed and Kara had helped lay each one on a bed of lush, black silk. Nan thought that, in a wonderful way, they told the story of what she now saw as their crazy, amazing summer together.

Ms. Webster joined them for a moment, putting her arms around as many of them as she could.

"So, what do you think, kids?" she asked. Kara beamed up at her mother.

"Very impressive," came a soft, thin voice from behind them.

"Grandma Douglas!" Kara exclaimed, running to wrap her arms around the frail old woman in her wheelchair.

"Careful," said Samantha Douglas, who had been pushing from behind.

"Oh, she's just fine, Sammi," Grandma Douglas said, clearly happy to see them all.

Samantha gushed. "The place is just gorgeous!"

Ms. Webster put her hand on Samantha's shoulder. "Shall we tell them?" she asked, coyly.

Nan was just as surprised as everyone else to see her mom be so chummy with the librarian, of all people. She didn't even know they knew each other!

"We're moving in!" Samantha burst out.

Nan was shocked. "Oh my gosh," she said.

The others started chatting away with excitement at the surprise.

"Cool," said Ace.

Nan smiled. More of her mom's magic!

"We can't wait," said Samantha. "It just couldn't have worked out any better!"

Grandma Douglas turned her focus back to the display case. "Just look at all those rocks! Kara, I see you included my little contribution."

"I did!" Kara said proudly. "Aren't they so pretty?"

"They sure are," Samantha agreed. "And I really like the theme you chose."

"Theme?" Nan asked, bewildered. She looked at the rocks again.

"Sure," Samantha answered. "It's kind of a 'stepping stones to wealth' theme. They all seem to be connected to me."

A sea of faces turned back to take another look at Kara's rocks, their words jumping out at them from the sparkling glass case in a whole new way.

"If you read these rocks one right after another," Samantha commented, "they all link together. It's as if they form a plan for finding that treasure you were looking for. If you follow the rocks, you can reach your dreams!"

"Rocks to riches..." Nan murmured under her breath.

"What?" Ms. Webster asked.

"Rocks to riches," Nan spoke up, repeating herself. "They *are* like stepping stones...you follow the rocks to riches."

"I love that!" Ms. Webster said with a smile. "And, what better place to display them than at Rockworth Manor?"

Nan looked up at her mother, returning the smile. Her mother had been following the steps all along. And so had they. Everything they had done this past summer had brought them here! She glanced around at the beautiful surroundings and felt yet another surge of pride.

★ ★ ★ ★ ★

The front doors swung open, and a flow of people entered the lobby.

"I guess that's my cue," Ms. Webster said, slipping away to meet her newest guests.

"We're going to go up and have another look at our apartment," Samantha said. "The movers are bringing our things over this weekend, and we need to decide where to put the furniture."

"You kids go check out the refreshment table," Grandma Douglas said with a wink.

Nan watched as Samantha wheeled Grandma Douglas toward the elevator. She loved the idea of having them at Rockworth Manor. She felt like her little family was growing, and it felt really good.

Lost in her daydream, Nan didn't notice the others had gone to get food until she felt Ace's hand grabbing hers and pulling her along. Her stomach rose into her chest with a flutter.

"Come on," he said. "It's a great spread!"

She drew in a breath, feeling like she'd never breathe again.

When they reached the table, however, Ace let go of her hand to get a plate. She sighed with happiness *and* disappointment.

"This is great!" said Jack through a mouthful of chocolate-covered strawberry. He had already loaded his plate with one of everything.

Nan made a plate for herself and joined her friends on a long, low bench in a corner of the lobby. As they ate, they watched Ms. Webster flutter about like a butterfly, greeting her guests and sending them off to tour the building with Mr. Medlin and Mrs. Davis.

Nan scowled as Millie noisily gobbled down a sandwich. "Jeez, Millie! Why don't you taste it before you swallow it?"

"What just got into you, Nan?" retorted Millie. "Everything is perfect!"

Nan shook her head, realizing Millie was right. Everything *was* perfect!

"Sorry, momentary lapse of happiness!" Nan joked.

Millie laughed and took an even bigger bite of the sandwich which oozed out the sides of her mouth, sending them all into hysterics!

Nan couldn't remember exactly why she had been so jealous of Millie. Looking back, she saw just how miserable Millie had been despite all of the things that she used to own. She was definitely much happier now, and didn't whine anywhere near as much as she used to. It occurred to Nan that she and Millie had both grown up and conquered a few fears over the summer. Nan was no longer afraid of being poor, and Millie was no longer afraid to let people know that she might be less than perfect.

"Fears are just negative fantasies," Nan thought, repeating to herself another of her mother's favorite sayings.

"So, Millie…" Ace mumbled through a mouthful of cookie crumbs. "How did your rummage sale go?"

"Really good," she said, wiping her lips with a napkin. "I don't know why we didn't do it sooner. We actually made quite a bit of money, and I even opened my own savings account. I'm thinking about having a rummage sale every year! I mean, why keep all that useless junk around when you could sell it and do something good with it?"

"It's too bad we couldn't start a business selling used junk," Jack said.

"Why couldn't we?" Ace asked him.

"Yeah, why couldn't we?" Kara piped up.

Nan's face lit up as an idea took hold in her brain. "You know…" she said thoughtfully. The others looked toward her, waiting for her to continue.

"There's still that empty space at the front of the building with all the windows…maybe we could set up a little shop in there. We could sell our own stuff, but we could also help other people sell theirs."

"That's a great idea!" Ace said. Nan could see the wheels turning in his head, too, as their plan began to form.

"You know what would be even better?" Millie prompted. "We could ask people to donate things, and then after we sell them, we could use part of the money to help people who need it. Maybe we could help people who are having money problems like my family. When they come in, we could show them Kara's rocks and teach them how to make a plan to help themselves!"

"That would be awesome!" Jack said, grinning at Millie.

As much as he had liked the old Millie, Nan thought he was growing even fonder of the new one.

Jack took off his trusty backpack. "I have just what we need to start writing our plan!" he said with authority.

Nan waited for Ace to say something sarcastic about Jack, but he didn't. He just kept eating.

* * * * *

Nan was only half paying attention to the directions Jack was giving out about their new plan. She was straining to listen to the conversation between her mom and Mrs. Medlin.

"Who is that?" she heard Mrs. Medlin ask.

Nan looked to see a tall, handsome man who had just entered the building. Nan watched him pause to survey the lobby in an approving sort of way.

Mrs. Medlin gave Ms. Webster a little shove. "Why don't you go see if you can help him with something?" she said coyly.

Nan watched her mom approach the man with a beautiful, flashing smile that shone from her eyes. "Welcome to Rockworth Manor," she said, extending her hand to the handsome stranger. "Unfortunately, we have leased all of our units, but I would be happy to put you on our waiting list just in case."

The man took her outstretched hand and smiled warmly. "You must be the fabulous Maureen Webster I have heard so much about," he said.

Nan's mom actually blushed! Nan couldn't remember if she had ever seen that before. She looked around to make sure her eavesdropping wasn't obvious and then moved in a little closer.

"Actually," the man said, "I'm not looking to lease an apartment. I just came to meet the woman who talked old Gisewski out of this building. How did you do it? I've been trying to buy this place from that old geezer for years, and he wouldn't ever give me the time of day!"

"Well, I had a very powerful ally," Ms. Webster replied.

"Oh?"

"*Mrs.* Gisewski."

They shared a laugh, and then a brief awkward silence which the handsome stranger broke.

"Well, I suppose I should introduce myself," he said. "I'm Martin Pierce. I own the apartment buildings on either side of you. And, I would like to thank you and congratulate you on your recent purchase. You see, my property value has taken a leap to the skies since you took over."

Ms. Webster extended her hand once again. "So nice to meet you, Mr. Pierce," she said pleasantly. This time the handshake appeared to last a few seconds longer than necessary. Nan's eyes felt like they were popping out of her head to get every detail.

"Well, I don't want to keep you from your party," Mr. Pierce continued, "but I wonder if I could take you out to dinner some time."

Nan gasped and slapped her hand over her mouth to stifle herself.

Mr. Pierce kept talking. "I have some ideas I'd love to discuss with you for some improvements I have wanted to make to the areas between our buildings."

"Of course," Ms. Webster replied. "I'll give you my card."

She stepped over to the lobby counter and retrieved a business card. Nan watched Martin Pierce watch her mother. She watched her mom pause a moment, then grab a pen and write on the back of her card.

"Here's my private number," she told Mr. Pierce, offering him the card. "Call me anytime."

Nan's mouth dropped open. She couldn't remember ever seeing her mother flirt before!

"I believe I will," he replied, bending to give her hand a gentlemanly kiss. "It was so nice to meet you. I must be going, but I hope this will be the beginning of a long and fruitful relationship."

"It was nice to meet you, Martin," her mom said. "Have a rest of the day."

Nan covered her face and peeked through her fingers. "Oh my gosh, oh my gosh, oh my gosh," she said to herself.

CHAPTER 18

# The Real Gold

Nan ran deeper into the autumn-colored woods behind Millie's old house, nearly at Jack's heels. She could easily outrun him but he'd had a head start. Apparently Jack had left his house earlier in the day after a stormy argument with his mom. No one had been too concerned about it until it started getting late, which is when Nan got Ace's call.

All three girls joined Ace and Mr. Emerson to spread out and search the woods behind Millie's old house. Nan was the one to spot him but, as soon as she did, he took off running.

She was close enough now to see the tears streaming down his face and could hear his stifled sobs. She knew he didn't want her to see him crying, but she didn't care at this point. Chubbs was lumbering behind Nan, moving as quickly as his oversized body could manage.

"Jack, stop," Nan pleaded. "We'll figure something out. Just stop."

Jack stopped when he reached the bank of the stream and turned to face Nan. Chubbs ran knee-deep into the stream and snuffled up a snout full of water.

"You didn't hear what she said," Jack sobbed. "'I'm sorry, Jack, but that pig just has to go,'" he said, imitating his mother.

"'We don't have the money to build him a barn for the winter. We have to send him someplace where he can be taken care of.' *That's* what she said, Nan. That's what she said."

"Jack, I know it seems hopeless right now but we'll do something. We'll sell things. We'll make it work. We will. Remember the rocks," she implored.

"*He* wasn't any help, either," Jack said, referring to Mr. Emerson. "He just kept saying that it would be too cold outside for Chubbs. If they're going to send Chubbs away, then I'm going too!"

"Jack, where are you?" Kara's voice floated through the woods. Nan looked back up the ravine and was relieved to see her come into view with Millie.

"Jack! Jeez!" Millie called.

"Jack, there you are!" Ace appeared over the edge of a small rise along the other side of the stream, and Jack scowled.

"Go away!"

"Come on, Jack!" Millie cried. "It's getting cold out here. Just come home and let's figure something out."

"What's to figure out?" he exclaimed. "If Chubbs has to go away, then I'm going with him!"

"Jack, you're being ridiculous," Ace said.

Nan tried to reason with him. "What are you going to do, live out here in the woods?"

"Maybe," Jack mumbled.

"Chubbsie, come back!" Kara cried, stumbling along the rocky bank after the fat pig, whose big behind was making a beeline downstream.

"Now what is he doing?" Millie cried, running after them. "Kara, slow down."

"Chubbs!" Jack called. "Oh, this is just great!"

Nan, Jack, and Ace took off after Chubbs, Kara, and Millie. They rounded a bend in the stream and nearly ran into each other.

"Why did you stop?" Ace yelled, barely managing to keep himself from falling into the water as he avoided stepping on Kara.

Kara couldn't speak, but merely pointed to a dark hole in the side of a small, rocky cliff.

"A cave!" Jack exclaimed. He wiped his nose on his sleeve. "Did Chubbs go in there?"

Kara and Millie nodded.

Jack and Ace ran to the small cave. Nan jumped across the rocks to join them. They looked inside. She could hear Chubbs breathing and snuffling, as his deep pig voice echoed off the rock walls. It was pitch black inside the cave, though, and they couldn't see a thing.

"What do you think he's doing in there?" Millie asked.

"Maybe he's smelling out another rock," Kara said hopefully.

The boys looked at each other, but neither of them seemed interested enough to go inside.

"Ace! Jack!"

Startled, they looked up to find Mr. Emerson peering over the edge of the cliff above them.

"There you are! What are you two doing? Where's Chubbs?"

The boys pointed into the cave, and Mr. Emerson ran swiftly down the hill toward them. He stopped and stared, too. Nan felt relieved now that he was here.

Suddenly, a hard, shiny, golden blob of a rock tumbled out of the cave, leaving a trail of dust behind it. It lay before them, glinting in the waning sunlight that filtered through the orange and gold leaves above them.

They stood and stared as Chubbs emerged from the cave with a triumphant look on his filthy swine face. Jack stepped forward and leaned down to pick up the rock. He held it up and examined it in the light.

"It's gold!" he said in astonishment.

"What?" Ace cried.

"It's gold!" Jack laughed through his tears. "Real gold!"

"We're rich!" Kara cried. The others laughed in amazement.

"Well, technically, Chubbs is rich," Ace joked. "After all, he's the one who found the gold."

"Yeah, Chubbs is rich," Jack repeated. "We can't very well get rid of a rich pig, now, can we?" He looked up at Mr. Emerson with a hopeful expression on his face.

"I don't know, Jack."

"Aw, come on, dad!" Ace pestered him. "You said the only reason we couldn't keep Chubbs is because we can't afford to build him a barn. Surely that chunk of gold is big enough to pay for a little, old barn!"

"Please, Mr. Emerson!" Kara begged. "Don't make Chubbs go away, I'll miss him so much!"

"We don't even know for sure if that's real gold," Mr. Emerson stalled.

"It is!" Jack exclaimed. "I know it is! I've been studying rocks for years, and I know how to tell the difference between real gold and fool's gold!"

"I don't know," Mr. Emerson was doubtful.

"Please, Mr. Emerson?" Millie begged.

"Please?" Nan joined in.

"Chubbs is a magic rock finder, Mr. Emerson!" added Kara.

Mr. Emerson stared at their pleading faces. "Your mother will have my neck," he said finally.

Jack threw his arms around his stepfather. "Oh, thank you!" He hadn't completely agreed to let Chubbs stay, but he had opened up enough room for a little faith to get in!

"Thanks, Dad," said Ace.

"Well, let's just find out for sure if this is real gold and, if it is, how much it's worth," Mr. Emerson told Jack sternly. "If we can sell it for enough money, we'll build Chubbs a little house in the back yard."

"Yay!" Kara jumped up and down excitedly, and the others grinned.

"Come on," Mr. Emerson told them. "Let's go home."

"Yeah," Jack agreed. "Come on, Chubbs, let's *all* go home!"

– The End (for now) –

# Stepping Stones to Wealth

(Rock Inscriptions)

# About the Authors

## Elisabeth Donati

Born and raised on farms in Michigan and Bend, Oregon, Elisabeth learned how to do just about everything...except what to do with money. Little did she know that once she taught herself, she would have a whole new career teaching others about money, investing and creating businesses they love.

Elisabeth is now the Pres./CEO of Creative Wealth Intl., LLC and creator of the innovative financial education programs Camp Millionaire, The Money Game®, Creative Cash for Kids and more. She trains people all over the globe to empower kids and teens to be responsible for themselves and the world. She is a very successful financial coach helping people with money and business.

After writing The Ultimate Allowance for parents, she decided to try her hand at a financial book for youth. Rocks to Riches is her first Kids' Financial Adventure, a genre she hopes will catch on as financial education becomes as commonplace as reading, writing, and arithmetic!

When she's not teaching, writing, or developing new programs, you can find Elisabeth in Santa Barbara, California, swimming, doing a bit of yoga, baking gluten-free muffins and cookies and tending her wine-barrel garden ~ the things she enjoys most!

Elisabeth likes to say that her purpose in life is inviting people to think differently about everything. Please read more about Elisabeth at www.ElisabethDonati.com

## Jan K. Ruskin

Jan has spent most of her professional life collecting experiences. Starting out in politics, then moving into film and television, education, and life coaching, she is now advocating for financial education. The common thread throughout has been writing, and Jan is thrilled to step into her dream of being a published author.

One of the things Jan loves most about writing is letting the characters tell their own story. In fact, it was actually Nan Webster who coaxed Jan into co-writing *Rocks to Riches.* Originally brought in as a copy editor, Jan ended up spending more of her time jotting down Nan's thoughts and ideas than correcting punctuation. Pretty soon, R2R became a collaborative project!

Jan lives in Santa Barbara, California with her husband, son, and two stepdaughters.

For more information about this book and additional resources for financial education, please contact:

Creative Wealth Intl., LLC

P. O. Box 91140
Santa Barbara, CA 93190
805-957-1024

www.RocksToRichesBook.com
www.CampMillionaire.com
www.WinTheMoneyGame.com

Elisabeth@CreativeWealthIntl.org

Jan@CreativeWealthIntl.org

CPSIA information can be obtained at www.ICGtesting.com
Printed in the USA
BVOW040556240812

298584BV00007B/7/P

9 780977 461844